Donut
Delivery!

Donut
Delivery!

Coco Simon

Simon Spotlight

New York London Toronto Sydney New Delhi

SIMON SPOTLIGHT

An imprint of Simon & Schuster Children's Publishing Division
1230 Avenue of the Americas, New York, New York 10020
This Simon Spotlight edition December 2021
Copyright © 2021 by Simon & Schuster, Inc.
All rights reserved, including the right of reproduction in whole or in part in any form.
SIMON SPOTLIGHT and colophon are registered trademarks of Simon & Schuster, Inc.
Text by Samantha Thornhill
For information about special discounts for bulk purchases, please contact Simon & Schuster Special Sales at 1-866-506-1949 or business@simonandschuster.com.
Designed by Ciara Gay
The text of this book was set in font.
Manufactured in the United States of America 1021 OFF
10 9 8 7 6 5 4 3 2 1
ISBN 978-1-6659-0079-9 (hc)
ISBN 978-1-6659-0078-2 (pbk)
ISBN 978-1-6659-0080-5 (ebook)
Library of Congress Catalog Card Number 2021946654

Chapter One
Freedom Week!

It was almost spring break at Bellgrove Middle School.

The flowers were starting to bloom, the birds were showing off their springtime symphonies, and the whole town was smiling and enjoying spending time outdoors again.

This was when long pants started to fade away, sweaters went on vacay, and school hallways were suddenly sprinkled with tank tops, skirts, and shorts.

Normally these early days of spring would be my favorite time of year, but this year I was feeling a little annoyed by the change in weather.

I think it had to do with the fact that I was in middle school now.

Was it wrong for me to want to feel a little more grown-up in my clothes, and in my overall appearance?

And springtime at Bellgrove Middle School was also when it became abundantly clear to everyone who was allowed to shave their legs, and who wasn't.

Can you guess which side of that fence I was stuck on?

My mom is the assistant principal of my school, and let's just say that despite her stylish and modern clothes, she has some unfair ideas on stuff.

How she got the idea that her daughters shouldn't start shaving their legs until they're in high school is so unfair!

When I asked her why I had to wait until I was in high school, what she told me was pretty simple.

My mom's mom, Grandma Rita, didn't let her daughters shave their legs until they were in high school.

That's it. That's the only reason.

Leave it to my mom to carry on tradition, I guess. . . .

As for my dad, he's pretty protective of me and my older sister and isn't exactly enthused about us looking too grown-up in any way, so he definitely had Mom's back on this one, like always.

"Mom, who cares if I have hair on my legs or not?" I tried to reason with her once.

Mom looked at me and smiled, like a cat who had just caught its evening meal.

"Exactly my point," she said. "So why go through all the trouble if no one cares? Who are you trying to impress anyway, Casey?"

"No one!" I said.

But that wasn't 100 percent true, was it?

Mom got me thinking. I'd had hair on my legs for some time now. Why did I want to shave all of a sudden?

Was it because the other girls my age were doing it? Or did I want to shave my legs for another reason?

My older sister, Gabby, who's now in her first year of community college, went through the same thing with this rule all through middle school.

By the time she got to high school, she was one of the last girls in her class with unshaved legs.

Lucky for her, Gabby refused to wait.

I love how Gabby tells the story about the morning she gracefully rebelled. She and Mom were out grocery shopping for family Saturday brunch.

This was a few years ago, right before Gabby was going to enter high school. They were doing self-checkout, the ones where you scan your own groceries.

Right in front of our mom's face, Gabby took a packet of disposable razors. She then scanned it and put it into the bag, watching Mom the entire time she did so.

The way she tells it, Mom gave her this strange look she'd never seen before, or since, and never said another word about it.

Gabby's had beautifully smooth legs ever since.

But that's my sister Gabby for you. Being a straight-A student and a talented dancer means she can sometimes color outside the lines and know she'll get away with it.

Being an average student and all, I just don't see myself getting away with half the things Gabby does. I can't see myself being bold enough to do what Gabby did.

I told Lindsay Mom would be all over me if I even glanced at a pack of razors.

Speaking of my BFF, what I looked forward to

the most about spring break was getting to spend the whole week with Lindsay. We always plan out every day of our spring breaks, down to the last second.

It's the one week we feel like we're free to do what we want, when we want.

That's how we came to call spring break our "Freedom Week." Since we were little kids, we've spent as many of our spring breaks together as we possibly could.

We've even had our parents agree to a few sleepovers during Freedom Week.

Actually, this has been going on since we were babies, because of our moms.

Back then, our moms planned our spring breaks, since they both worked at the school and had off at the same time.

Then, the four of us would spend almost all our spring breaks together, every year. We would watch movies, do projects, and later, go on hikes. Fun times!

As soon as we got to decision-making age, whenever that was, our moms left it up to us to plan our spring breaks.

So that's the long and short of how Freedom Week was born. Usually during Freedom Week we've kept up the tradition of doing fun art projects and geeking out on our favorite movies.

But this year, now that we were in middle school, I wanted to level up and do different stuff!

For instance, I wanted to incorporate some acting exercises that we did in camp last summer.

I couldn't wait to tell Lindsay about my ideas for Freedom Week.

On the Friday before spring break, I walked into the school lunchroom and headed straight for our usual table in the center, close to where the girls' soccer and field hockey teams sat.

Lindsay is no athlete and neither am I. She is a no-nonsense working girl, and I'm an artist.

We didn't really fit into one particular group, so our table was a hodgepodge of girls with some different and overlapping interests: our friend Michelle, who's a photographer, Lindsay's new friend Maria, whose family opened a cool Puerto Rican bakery in town; and Melanie Fox, a friend of Lindsay's from her art class.

Overall, lunch was a pretty cool scene.

Today, Lindsay was the first one at our lunch table. Perfect timing!

I liked when we could grab some moments alone before the other girls swooped in with their raucous laughter and hilarious dramas.

"Hey, tuna on rye," I said, sitting down.

"What's up, leftover lasagna," she answered back.

Lindsay had tuna on rye and I had, well, leftover lasagna.

We smiled knowingly at each other, because it was a comfort to know someone and be known so well. We always knew what the other was having based on the day of the week.

I noticed Lindsay was jotting something on a piece of paper. When she finished, she raised her catlike green eyes to me and smiled.

"I've been brainstorming a list of movies that we can watch this week," she said.

"About Freedom Week," I said. "I was thinking we could watch movies along a certain theme."

"Like what?"

"What do you think of anime?" I asked.

Lindsay's eyes slid back down to her paper.

"I have a couple animes on here, but not a week's worth," she said. "Maybe we can have an anime . . . day.

"Oh, how about this . . . each day we have a different movie theme? We can even have a scary movie night!" she added excitedly.

"Great idea, Linds," I said. "I don't know when I became such an anime fan anyhow."

"Yeah, what's up with that?" Lindsay asked.

When I didn't say anything right away, she filled in the blanks.

"Let me guess . . . Matt Machado?" Lindsay asked in a syrupy, singsong voice.

It had taken me a while to admit it, but Matt Machado was legit my first crush.

I had met him at sleepaway camp last summer, and we became the best of friends.

We weren't old enough to be anything more than that, but if we were allowed to date, I wonder if we would be something more.

I wasn't exactly sure how Matt or even I felt about that.

"Okay, Matt loves anime and now I'm hooked," I admitted, holding my head in my hands and groaning.

Lindsay giggled.

"Hooked on anime . . . or Matt?" she asked.

I blushed, and Lindsay waved it off.

"You're hopeless. Anyhow, let me know which animes you want to watch this week to add to the list," she said.

"You're the best, Linds," I told her. "I can't wait for our glorious week of freedom."

"Same here. It's my favorite time of year because of you," Lindsay said. "I also love how we're carrying on something that our moms started."

A moment of silence followed. I knew it was because we were both thinking about Lindsay's mom, Amy Cooper, who had joined the angels.

I also thought about how much we could use this quality time.

Middle school had been hard on our friendship, especially since I came back from camp all boy crazy and artsy—two sides of me Lindsay had never seen before.

It put us in a sort of funky space for a while, but we'd worked through things.

Still, we didn't exactly have the same level of comfort that we'd had before, and I was hoping that Freedom Week would help us to get it back.

I was also looking forward to taking my mind

off Matt. He lives five hours away in a town called Hardwick.

I thought of him constantly . . . the memories we shared at camp, his handsome face burned into my mind, all the laughter we'd shared.

From what Matt's mom told me (I talked to her a few times on the phone), Matt sounded pretty into me, too.

She said they talk about me all the time.

As I rattled off some anime titles for Lindsay to write down, I gazed at my oldest friend in the world.

Lindsay knew almost everything about me.

Almost.

While she wrote, I admired the river of reddish-brown hair flowing down her shoulders.

When I say Lindsay's my oldest friend, that's real talk. We were born a day apart and first met in the hospital nursery.

Our moms were work friends before we came along, but having babies at the same time formed a bond between them that has outlasted Amy Cooper's death.

Somehow, my mom still feels really connected to Lindsay's mom, even though she's no longer here.

My mom says she can still feel her friend's gentle, loving presence in the hallways at school.

Something that Lindsay and I used to have in common was our take on boys.

After all, Bellgrove boys had been grossing us out on the regular since kindergarten. Our vibe was to hate their guts until further notice.

Then I experienced something different at camp when I met Matt. He was different from any other boy I'd ever met.

First of all, he looked and smelled really good.

Also, he wasn't some undercover or outright video-game addict. Instead he had this black notebook that he took with him everywhere, because he was always writing stuff down that he saw, thought, and experienced.

He was really interested in a bunch of stuff, and all the adults at camp adored him because he could talk about anything.

He looked up subjects he wanted to learn about and didn't try to act dumb or tough to fit in like other boys.

Matt was also in touch with his feelings.

I remember him getting pretty emotional when

he talked about his mom marrying his stepdad years back.

That was when his last name was legally changed to Machado.

Also, Matt's biracial, just like me.

This was something we had in common at camp, so it drew us closer together right away.

His biological dad, who left when Matt was two, was white, and his mom is black and from the Caribbean.

My parents, however, are the reverse: my dad's black and my mom's white.

Besides my sister, Matt's the only person who I know totally gets me for me.

The lunchroom was beginning to fill up. I knew we wouldn't be alone at this table for much longer.

Lindsay had to raise her voice in order for me to hear her.

"Matt sounds like a pretty cool guy. I'd love to meet him someday," she said.

"Yessss! That would be fire! We should call him on video chat sometime," I said.

I was excited at the thought.

I wanted Lindsay to understand just what I saw

in Matt, and I wanted Matt to put a face and a voice to the BFF I'd so often spoken about back at camp.

"Cool!" Lindsay agreed.

Even though I was just about the only thing Lindsay and Matt had in common, I pictured them totally hitting it off.

Lindsay loves meeting new people.

Unlike me, she's the type of small-town girl who wants to someday leave Bellgrove for big-city life and melt into the crowd and make a name for herself doing some awesome and unpredictable things.

It took Lindsay a little while to adjust to my changes.

Even though she's accepted Matt's place in my life, I still caught her giving me these looks when I did certain things or when I brought him up a lot.

Like when my phone lit up with a text message, and I would grab it like it was my favorite candy bar that suddenly appeared out of thin air.

I never used to do that before last summer, so it was always pretty obvious to Lindsay that it had to do with Matt.

I guess to her I had to look pretty obsessed. But I didn't think I was that bad.

It was also kind of embarrassing to be honest because Matt hardly texted me anyhow.

That was another thing. . . . Matt and I were so connected at camp, but as soon as we were back into our regular lives, he went dark.

AWOL.

MIA.

At first I thought it was because he had lost interest in me, but that turned out to be some fiction I created in my mind.

After weeks of not knowing what was up with this boy and his late one-word responses to all my texts, I finally caught up with him one night and we texted for a good while.

That was when I found out that he was thinking about me every day too.

He was just super busy and was always getting his phone taken away by his mom for disciplinary reasons.

So it wasn't what I had thought at all!

The only thing that was really keeping us apart besides geography were my own doubts about myself.

Those silly voices in my head that whispered

harsh nothings that I began to believe: that last summer, to Matt, was just a fluke, a friendship that meant nothing to him.

Hanging out with me was just a way to pass the time before he could return to his more exciting, regularly scheduled life.

The morning after we'd texted, Matt and his mom called during our Saturday brunch. It was fun but super awkward at points.

Dad learned just how much I hadn't been hanging out with only girls at sleepaway camp. And I learned just how much his mom knew about me, like my intense love of cat memes! And my mom learned how much she was dying to have a new friend her age just to chop it up with.

Matt's mom and mine got along so famously that they ended up exchanging numbers soon after.

Matt's mom looked like an actual queen, with her mocha skin, braids, and long neck.

However, I didn't let that warm, glowing smile of hers fool me.

I happened to know from Matt that she was a super disciplinarian and was no-nonsense about his education.

The way he described her made my mom seem like Mary Poppins. With his mom always over his shoulder, he had no time for much outside of school and extracurricular activities.

When I found out that his mom took his phone from him for days at a time so he could focus on school, I felt so stupid for feeling all rejected and in my feelings for no reason.

I'd immediately assumed that he'd stopped caring about me, when he was actually phoneless and slaving over his schoolwork.

I swear, the next time that sneaky negative voice worms its way into my brain, that voice that says I'm not good enough, or not likeable, or not this, or not that, I'm going to face it head-on and tell it to go away!

After that first chat at brunch, Matt and I started talking more on video chat.

And each time we did, it felt like no time had passed since we were last together. It was like he was right there with me. It was kind of weird and cool at the same time.

Now that Matt and I had come to a better understanding and I'd been reminded of his amazingness, I began to miss my friend more than I had in the first place. I guess that was when he officially became my crush.

The rest of our friends showed up to our table, so it was too late to spill my guts to Lindsay.

I was hooked on Matt more than I wanted to be, and I needed some advice on how to cure myself of this boy disease.

It was no use bringing this stuff up to any of my friends, who all saw boys as annoying creatures.

My sister was the only one who would really understand.

Even though I tried not to run to Gabby for every single thing, she was basically my personal guru about life matters, and she always taught me so much.

I hadn't gone to her in a while about anything, and this conversation was long overdue.

I made a mental note to go see her when I came home from school.

I couldn't wait until the school day was over.

Chapter Two

I Love My Sister, But . . .

As soon as I got home, I made a beeline for Gabby's room and knocked once before bursting in.

I found her in her usual predicament, trying to decide between two different outfits for some occasion or other.

"Right on time!" Gabby said, grinning.

She always asked for my advice on her outfits, since I have an eye for what looks good.

I stood behind her as she gazed at herself in front of her mirror, an outfit dangling from each hand.

They looked a little more professional than her usual party outfits.

Right then and there, I couldn't help but take in my sister's swanlike beauty.

Of all the girls at Bellgrove High, Gabby has the darkest skin, with the brightest smile this side of the moon.

She doesn't look like she has a white mom at all.

For as long as I could remember, I'd admired the certainty of Gabby's dark-chocolate skin and wanted a color just as rich and brown as hers.

Meanwhile, Gabby adored my confused peanut butter complexion with killer curls.

I guess the grass is always greener on the other side.

Since I'm a lighter shade of brown, I haven't had the same struggles as Gabby.

I don't remember anyone in our hometown ever treating me as less than because of my blackness.

But it hasn't always been as easy for my darker sister to feel the true sense of belonging that I have felt here all my life.

She's been called names, not invited to birthday parties, and more. I've only caught hints of her experiences because she's protected me from most of them, and in general doesn't talk about them much.

I wish she spoke up about these things more.

Then maybe I'd be more sensitive, aware . . . and prepared.

Still, despite some difficult experiences, my big sister is hands down the most lovable girl in all of Bellgrove.

I can't imagine anyone not wanting to be around her just because she's noticeably darker.

It's like this quote that I read somewhere from this black writer, Zora Neale Hurston: if someone didn't want to be around her just because of the color of her skin, then there was something wrong with them for not wanting to bask in her company.

Or something like that.

That's how I felt about Gabby. If anybody didn't want to be around her, it was absolutely their loss.

But deep down I knew that wasn't exactly how Gabby felt about herself.

No matter how much she succeeded at things, she was always driven to do it better the next time.

Sometimes I wondered who she was really trying to please or what she was trying to prove.

She was all-around beautiful, brilliant, and a great friend to anyone in need.

She kicked butt at everything she did.

Grades.

Ballet.

Cooking.

I mean, the girl could sew and code!

Gabby whipped around and gestured to her two outfits. One was a knee-length satin floral dress with an empire waist, and the other was a chic pin-striped jumpsuit.

"Which one do you think is more appropriate for the first university tour?" Gabby asked.

"What university tour?" I asked.

I mean, it was true that Gabby was now thinking about going away to college.

At first she wanted to live at home, which thrilled my parents, but after a year of her friends telling her how great it was to live in a dorm, she was ready for a big change.

She said she was thinking about living on campus, but I didn't know squat about a tour.

"Oh, nobody told you?" Gabby asked. "Girl, you need to get it together. Someone must've mentioned it to you at some point. Where's your head these days?"

She and I both knew the answer to that.

And between Mom's busy schedule at our middle school and Dad's epic adventures at the clinic, it would have been easy for that memo to slip through the cracks.

Gabby rolled her eyes and continued. "Well, start packing, girl. We're going away this weekend for a week of college tours. Yippee!"

My sister looked like she was going to burst with glee.

Who could blame her? She was about to be a new fish in a sea of other new fish. Boy fish.

Gabby felt nothing but joy, but as for me, a lump was forming in my throat at the thought of my big sister not living right across the hall the way she has my entire life.

I took a good look around, and Gabby in fact was actively and certifiably . . . packing . . . for a road trip!

"Oh no!" I exploded, once the news had started to sink in.

"That's tomorrow! Why do I have to go? Lindsay and I had our whole spring break week planned out. She's going to be crushed!" I cried.

"Lindsay might be your BFF, but I'm your sister,

and I need you more this week than she does!" Gabby said.

She sighed before she continued.

"I'm going to college for the first time, for goodness' sake! I want to share this experience with you, too, not just our parents—how wack would that be if I left you out?"

"Facts," I had to agree.

Now that got me.

I couldn't do my big sis like that.

"Come on, Case," she drilled me. "You can geek out on *Goonies* and *Goosebumps* with Lindsay anytime. Besides, she had to go on a Casey fast for a good portion of last summer.

"What's a measly week? Your BFF is gonna be all right."

Gabby turned back to the mirror to scrutinize each outfit.

Suddenly, she asked, "Oh wait, did you need anything else, Case?"

"Forget it," I murmured.

I turned on my heel and closed her door behind me.

Chapter Three
No Way Out

At dinner that evening, I sure had a bone to pick with my parents.

For as long as I could remember, they'd let me—no, made me—choose how I spent my spring break, and it was always with Lindsay.

It was our freest week of the school year, hence the name "Freedom Week."

We're talking movie marathons, games, arts and crafts, and cheddar-cheese-and-caramel popcorn.

We even masterminded some of our own meals!

How were they just going to take that from me without saying a single word?

I wondered if I was being unfair.

After all, this week was really not about me.

This was Gabby's moment, and I got that.

I just didn't think it was fair for me to fall through the cracks, like my opinion or feelings didn't matter.

I couldn't help but feel some kind of way about finding out that my week of freedom had been dragged out from under me like a rug.

It felt like a slap in the face from my whole family.

I took a few deep breaths like Gabby taught me, to clear out some of the intensity of my emotions.

Before telling Lindsay about this big wrench in our plans, I wanted to see if I could get permission from my parents to stay in Bellgrove with the Coopers for the week.

Bold move, but possible.

Years ago, when my parents went on an anniversary Caribbean cruise during spring break, Gabby stayed with one of her friends, and I got to sleep over Lindsey's house for that whole week!

Now that was a Freedom Week for the books.

Imagine pajama days and pillow fights and feathers every which way. Then moaning and groaning through the whole cleanup the next day.

If the Coopers wouldn't mind hosting me for

another Freedom Week, and my parents were okay with it, we could save spring break after all.

Also, I definitely wasn't exactly jumping up and down to tell Lindsay that all the time we'd spent planning our perfect week was about to swirl down the drain.

"A whole university tour planned right under my nose!" I said in disbelief, using just a dash of humor to balance out my angst.

One thing I'd learned about my parents was that emotions did not move them . . . only logic did.

It was a challenge to keep my voice steady.

Thanks to Gabby's breathing exercises, I came into this conversation prepared.

As unsupportive to Gabby as it might sound, I was not interested in seeing one university, much less a string of them.

Everyone around the table seemed so excited with what was about to go down.

So much so that no one seemed to care how I really felt about being cooped up in a car for hours and days just to go gawk at a bunch of old buildings.

"I can't believe how this news got to me!" I said. I took a deep breath.

"I thought I had the choice to do what I wanted this week. But not only was that choice taken from me, I wasn't even told like a true member of this family. Who am I to you all really?" I finished dramatically.

Okay, maybe I was going a bit too far.

"Casey—" Mom started.

"Oh, the drama!" Gabby teased, rolling her eyes.

"Now I'll be the first to apologize to you because you do have a point, Case," said Mom. "We did discuss it briefly at dinner, but you must have not been listening.

"In the end, though, the decision was made behind closed doors.

"Your dad and I got our lines crossed on getting the news out, I guess."

"Lines crossed?" I asked. "We drive to school together every morning. How could it not have come up?"

Mom sighed. "You're right—I had many opportunities to bring it up. I'm not sure why I spaced on something so important.

"I know how much this week means to you and Lindsay both—boy, do I.

"Please send my apologies to Lindsay for the sudden change of plans."

"Aww, come on . . . why the long face, Case?" Gabby asked. "I always saw you as being down for any adventure—"

"Down like four flat tires," my dad chimed in.

"Well, not this time," I answered, avoiding Gabby's piercing eyes.

I saw my mom and dad lock eyes.

That usually happens when their conversation goes telepathic.

It was time to drop the question and let the chips fall where they may.

"Would you consider letting me stay at Lindsay's house this week, like you did the year of the cruise?" I asked.

"Ouch. Tell me how you really feel, Case," Gabby mumbled.

I glanced at her and was taken aback by how hurt she seemed.

Now Gabby didn't normally wear her heart on her face like I did, but if anyone could read Gabby's face like a book, it was me.

I knew her every feature, and her face was

definitely carrying this wounded expression.

I admit, it did soften me up a little. The last thing I ever wanted to do was hurt my big sister.

"That's a negative," Dad said, putting the smackdown on my half-cooked scheme to save Freedom Week.

He sighed. "This will be our first family trip in eons. You know how difficult it was for me to get an entire week off from the clinic this time of year? What about my Freedom Week?"

Dad had a point there. He really was the most hardworking dad in Bellgrove.

Outside of this dinner table, we hardly got to do things as a family anymore.

And now with Gabby planning to go away to college . . . welp!

"I guess I was only thinking about myself . . . and Lindsay," I admitted, with a sigh. "Middle school has been kicking my butt.

"We always have so much homework and stuff to do after school that Lindsay and I have no time for each other or our other interests.

"I haven't had time to take pictures or draw anymore!"

Not to mention that after school, Lindsay sometimes had to work at Donut Dreams, the donut shop inside her family's restaurant, the Park View.

I occasionally worked there on some weekends or during the week when they needed me to fill in for one of Lindsay's cousins.

It didn't feel like a job, especially when we got to try one of Nans's (that's Lindsay's grandma) new donut flavors.

She's the creative genius behind Donut Dreams.

"Don't be such a spring break Grinch, Casey," Mom said lightly. "Change is in the air. Can't you smell it?

"Your sister is taking a giant step into the unknown here. Would you consider being a little more supportive? This trip could be very grounding for her.

"Besides, why would we want to create all these new family memories without you? This will also be a great opportunity for you to look at colleges too.

"It's never too early to start thinking about this important stuff."

I didn't want to break it to my mom that seeing

a bunch of universities hours away from home was the last thing on my mind—that is, until I'd gone into Gabby's room for boy advice.

But everyone was right in what they were saying. It is what it is, and sometimes life gives you no choice but to go with the flow.

I mean, I could make everyone miserable with how displeased I was, but I was not about to be that girl!

Finally Gabby spoke up.

"I know you'd rather spend time with Lindsay next week than with us, and I get that. But I'm your sister, and this trip is a pretty big deal for me. This only happens once in a lifetime, not once a year.

"Plus, how will I remember all the colleges we visit without your great photography to document these amazing moments?"

It cheered me up a little to remember that as an artist I could actually serve a purpose on this trip, rather than just take up space in the car.

Looked like it was high time to dust off my lucky camera, anyhow.

Okay.

My mind was officially changed.

I was going to go into this weeklong trip all smiles and with bells on.

I apologized to my family for my glum attitude and promised to do better.

Everyone rejoiced and looked relieved.

"It'll be fun, kiddo," said Dad. "It'll be just like old times! We can sing those songs you like in the car."

"Dad, those were from when I was a little kid!" I groaned.

"That only speaks to how long it's been since we've done this," Mom pointed out.

Unbelievable. I came into this dinner hoping to sway my parents.

I didn't expect them to sway *me*!

After washing up the dishes, I went upstairs and texted Lindsay to see if she could talk for a few.

"OMG, I was *just* about to text you too!" Lindsay replied.

Lindsay called me.

"Guess what?" she said. "I have to work at Donut Dreams every day next week to fill in for my cousins. They're going on some college tour!"

I guess I shouldn't have been surprised.

Donut Delivery!

Lindsay has a couple of cousins around Gabby's age who are also going to be applying to colleges.

The cool thing about the Park and Donut Dreams is that almost all her cousins, aunts, and uncles work at one or the other.

I am the only nonfamily member that they've allowed into the family business.

Lindsay's grandfather, Grandpa Coop, always liked to say that I was one of the family, and every time I walked into the Park wearing my bright yellow Donut Dreams shirt, I sure felt like it.

"NOOO WAAAY," I said. "Well, I was going to tell you that I can't do Freedom Week either."

Now it was Lindsay's turn to say, "NO WAY!"

"Yeah way!" I said. "Gabby is going on a college tour too and needs a personal photographer."

"What a diva!" Lindsay half joked.

Sometimes, I could sense this silent competition between my BFF and my sister. Neither of them said anything mean to or about each other outright, but a competitive energy would come out in their words and tones at times.

"I'm happy for you and *sooo* jealous. I love road trips!" said Lindsay.

"I could use a little time away. Grandpa said that sales are a little down at Donut Dreams lately, and he's making us all go nutty trying to think of ways to get more sales," she added.

"How can sales be down at Donut Dreams?" I asked. "They're the best donuts ever!"

"They're not down a *lot*," Lindsay said. "Just enough for Grandpa to notice. I guess people try different desserts, and some people move away.

"Remember the Bowen family with their six kids? They used to come in all the time, and they moved recently.

"And remember Tina Balzano and Vivian Musico? They were best friends and would come in almost every day after school for a donut.

"Now they're both away at college. It's tough losing regulars like that, but what can you do?"

"Ugh. There has to be a way to drum up more sales. I bet if we put our minds to it—"

"Casey!" my mom called from downstairs. "Remember it's an early day tomorrow!"

"Okay, Mom, I'm almost off!" I said.

When I came back on the phone, Lindsay was calling to her dad.

"I'm almost finished, Dad!"

Lindsay's dad takes limiting cell-phone time seriously.

She wasn't even allowed to sleep with her phone in her room!

She had to leave her phone downstairs next to her dad's.

"Let's squeeze in a movie night before school starts up again," I said.

"You always have the best ideas," said Lindsay. "Okay. Gotta go. Have an amazing week. You'll have to tell me everything!"

"No doubt!" I said.

After I brushed my teeth and changed into my pj's, I turned off my phone for the night and plugged it in. I settled into my sheets, clicked off the light, and closed my eyes in the dark.

Since Lindsay wasn't exactly crying over our shattered plans, I gave myself permission to start getting hyped about the week ahead.

Mostly, I felt relieved that Lindsay wasn't exactly going to be sitting around twiddling her thumbs while I was off gallivanting all over the state with my family.

Before drifting off to sleep, I used this good habit of Gabby's called visualization.

It's kind of like daydreaming events that you want to happen into being.

I imagined capturing my sister's college visit like a real professional photographer, making her look like a rock star.

With those thoughts in mind, I drifted off to sleep with a big old smile on my face.

Chapter Four

Big Sis Beauty Treatment

I woke up early the next morning to put the finishing touches on my packing job for the weeklong trip.

Naturally, the first thing I reached for was my art bag.

I'd have hours with no homework, BFF, or movies, so inspiration was sure to strike.

I packed my sketchbook, thick drawing paper, and some graphite sketch pencils.

Most of my sketches had been in black and white, but I'd been wanting to start experimenting with color, it being spring and all.

So I packed my color pencils too, just in case.

I took my trusty camera bag off the hook behind my closet door and checked to make sure my batteries were all charged up and that my camera, lenses, and cords were arranged comfortably in the cushiony black bag.

Unlike my fashionista sister, who'd spent hours choosing at least two outfits for every day of this trip, I was cool with just tossing a few essentials into my small suitcase.

I don't work hard at how I show up in the world; anything I put together looks pretty okay on me as long as it's not pink.

It was supposed to be beautiful outside today, so I pulled on my tan blouse and an emerald-green skirt that fell just above the knee.

I trotted downstairs to the kitchen, where my mom was packing cheese paste sandwiches into a cooler bag, and Dad was making fruit salad.

"Mom, can we please stop by Donut Dreams before blowing outta town?" I asked.

I knew that Lindsay would be working this morning, and I really wanted to see her—and grab some of Nans's pillowy, sweet donuts for the car ride.

"We'll have to giddyup, but that's actually not a bad idea," Mom said.

Not a bad idea? I grinned.

Donut Delivery!

Like Lindsay says, I always have the best ideas!

My dad, who was chopping up pineapples and melons for what he named his vitamin salad, laughed.

Being the family and town doctor and all, he tries to keep us healthy, so we usually don't have too many sweets and treats in the house.

Today was an exception.

My parents knew they owed it to Lindsay, and to my taste buds, to swing through Donut Dreams for just a few minutes to show the Coopers some love.

"Gabby!"

Mom frowned as she called to the star of the show, who was upstairs in her room.

Gabby didn't answer.

Mom sent me a look that said, *Go upstairs to put out whatever fire is going on inside Gabby's brain and bring her downstairs.*

I trudged up the stairs.

I wasn't sure what I was expecting to see on the other side of Gabby's door, but it was good to know that my big sister had everything under control.

She was sitting on the floor in lotus position with all her bags packed, her eyes closed, hands resting lightly on her knees.

As a trained ballerina, she's had her share of ballet coaches over the years.

One in particular really helped Gabby to deal with her performance anxiety by instructing her to sit quietly in the dark by herself and focus on her breathing as she visualized the best possible outcome.

Gabby had been teaching me to meditate, but I wasn't good at it like she was.

Gabby could meditate in a car, in a crowded room, or even at a football game!

I had to be in the actual dark most of the time . . . so dark that I couldn't tell if my eyes were closed or open.

But meditating has helped me, too.

Gabby's eyes fluttered open when she heard me come in.

She smiled up at me, looking peaceful and ready. And not to mention gorgeous.

For this first college visit, she wore army-green jogger pants and a simple yellow blouse with a sweetheart neckline.

"You look supercute, Case," she said, looking me up and down.

Then she wrinkled her nose.

"Let's hook up those legs, though."

Gabby reached into her beauty drawer and pulled out a bottle of lotion and a big paintbrush.

"My legs? What are you—" I asked.

She placed her index finger to her lips.

"This is a don't ask, don't tell kind of situation," she said. "You'll either slap or thank me later."

She began to apply the thick lotion to my legs with the brush.

I felt like a canvas being painted on. It felt tickly, and also cool and kind of nice.

"Okay, I'll go downstairs and stall the parents. Stay here and keep this goop on for ten minutes, then rinse.

"If Mom notices, tell her that you borrowed some of my lotion and didn't know what it was.

"Got it?" Gabby said.

"Notices what? And what kind of lotion is it?" I asked, confused.

"Casey!" Gabby said.

"Sorry. Got it," I said.

Gabby scooped up her luggage and glided down the stairs.

I waited around, fiddling with my phone, and

then, after some time had gone by, went to the bathroom to rinse off the lotion.

Yikes, it had been more like fifteen minutes!

I'd kind of lost track in the vortex of my phone.

In the hallway I could hear Gabby downstairs in the kitchen freestyling excuses for my slow return.

I sat on the edge of our clawfoot tub and rinsed off the foamy lotion.

When it cleared away, I gasped!

My legs were silky smooth!

What kind of magical lotion had Gabby used on me?

I wanted to rejoice as the last of my dark leg hairs swirled down the drain.

Now I understood everything Gabby had been trying to warn me about before.

Would my mom notice my smooth legs?

What if she did?

I didn't want to throw Gabby under the bus, but I wasn't the best fibber, either.

I considered changing into sweatpants to avoid any drama, but I rather liked the feel of rubbing my smooth legs together.

It was a new feeling.

My mom was destined to find out one way or another.

Oh well.

I'd cross that bridge when I got to it, I guess.

I grabbed my stuff and flew downstairs to meet the rest of my family as they were loading up the last of our bags into my dad's SUV.

"Everyone buckled up?" Mom asked.

"Next stop: Donut Dreams," said Dad.

He fiddled for just the right music for the start of our family road trip.

Within minutes we were pulling up to the Park View and walked into the smell of freshly fried donuts wafting from the kitchen, where Nans made her magic.

Grandpa Coop, the creator of the restaurant, sat at his usual station at the front, where he greeted all his customers before one of his grandchildren whisked them to their seats.

Crinkles around his eyes and hairy ears aside, at the sight of us his face broke into a warm smile.

When Grandpa Coop opened up the Park View decades ago, there were hardly any other restaurants in town.

A few had popped up since then, but this one has been going strong for the longest—all because of its delicious menu, of course.

"My favorite family in town!" said Grandpa Coop.

I knew he meant every word.

In all the time that I'd spent working and hanging out here, I'd never heard Grandpa Coop say this to any other family.

While managing a whole restaurant, mind you, he also always managed to make me feel like a special person in his life.

Dad hung back to chat with Grandpa Coop while Mom, Gabby, and I headed toward the Donut Dreams counter.

Lindsay and her cousin Kelsey were busy clearing out a morning wave of customers, serving up donuts when they were at their utmost softness.

My mouth began to water like crazy.

The excited wave of customers flowed out.

Lindsay's eyes went huge and she squealed when she saw us.

Kelsey waved energetically.

With the three of us being in the same grade,

just a few years from now all three of us might be going on this same college tour.

Now that was something to visualize and look forward to.

"Surprise!" I said.

I snuck behind the counter to give hugs.

"Good morning, family!" said Lindsay. "You look amazing, Casey! You too, Gabby."

"Thanks!" we said.

Lindsay looked me up and down.

"Is it just me or are your legs—"

"What's the newest donut flavor?" Gabby cut in.

She rushed to lean over the donut counter in one fluid movement that only a ballerina or a feline could pull off.

I saw her give Lindsay a bug-eyed glare that said *zip it.*

Lindsay caught the drift and got down to business.

"Well, Nans outdid herself and literally rolled out our healthiest donut to date!" she said.

She put on a big smile, falling into sales mode.

"Nans says one elderberry jelly donut a day keeps the doctor away," Kelsey said brightly, backing her up.

She gestured to the donut case to reveal Nans's newest darlings.

Lightly dusted with sugar and cooked to perfection, the donuts looked swollen with pure goodness.

"Did I hear elderberries?" asked Dad.

He had finished talking to Grandpa Coop and was now approaching the donut display.

I'd never heard my father become so enthusiastic about donuts.

"Elderberries are great supporters of the immune system. I stand corrected—donuts can have health benefits!"

All of us laughed. Leave it to my doctor dad to nerd out on donuts.

He glanced at Mom, who was already looking at him.

"We'll take a dozen of mostly those, and mix in some others," Mom said.

She then looked at me. "You and Gabby can also choose a donut each."

"You can have mine," Gabby whispered, elbowing me and winking.

Wow.

Donut Delivery!

This never happened!

I just about died with gratitude at that moment.

My family was going all out to make it up to me.

"They're all on the house!" a voice said, emerging from the kitchen.

"Nans!" I called to the donut expert.

Nans showed up at the counter like a queen; even her apron was artfully smeared with streaks of icing.

No matter how hot or busy the kitchen, Nans always managed to look so cool and unbothered, never a drop of sweat or a hair out of place.

Instead of paying, Dad stuffed a twenty-dollar bill in the tip jar on the counter, making Lindsay and Kelsey high-five each other.

I have to admit, even though I'd resigned myself to showing up for my sister for the college visits with my high vibes, I still was feeling left out.

I imagined how much fun Lindsay and Kelsey were going to have working together all week, and Lindsay was probably imagining having a week like mine.

Like I've said before, the grass is always greener.

The Coopers chatted with us for a couple more

minutes before it came time for us to hit the road.

The first university tour was two hours from now, and we were almost two hours away!

Before we left, with everyone's words and laughter swirling around in all directions, I hung back with Lindsay. Finally we had a few seconds alone.

"Hey, tell me you did not shave without permission!" Lindsay asked.

"And get scolded by my mother? No way!" I answered.

I briefly explained what had happened this morning with Gabby's magical lotion.

"Ooh, Gabby is going to get it when your mom finds out!" Lindsay said, her eyes lighting up.

"She'll handle Mom. She always does," I said, laughing.

"Now I officially want your legs!" Lindsay said. "Naturally beautiful and silky smooth."

Lindsay wasn't allowed to shave her legs yet, either.

We giggled.

I looked down at my shining brown legs that I was amazed Mom hadn't caught wind of by now.

Donut Delivery!

This time, I can honestly say that the grass wasn't greener on the other side.

Now I didn't want anyone's legs but mine.

Back in the car, Gabby was visibly excited for our next stop, University #1.

Like a total dork, she pulled out an old-school map with little stickers on every place she wanted to visit—restaurants, parks, you name it!

It switched my attitude back to a happy neutral.

Maybe we could make this whole week an experience to remember, after all.

Chapter Five
Surprises Are Both Good and Bad

We arrived at the first college, the one closest to Bellgrove, at the very start of the campus tour.

So I guess you could say we hit the ground walking.

We walked with a group of twenty-some college-bound kids and their families, so it was a pretty big crowd.

Some people brought their nice cameras to capture the architecture and trees, but most were on camera phones.

I had stupidly forgotten my camera in the trunk since we were in kind of a rush, but oh well.

Donut Delivery!

I had a week's worth of colleges to capture.

As long as I had my sketchbook and pencils, which were in my trusty messenger bag, I was good.

I have to say, even though the tour was given by a senior, the first afternoon tour was *B-O-R-I-N-G*.

His monotone voice reminded me of my history teacher, Mr. Gilmore, who always managed to make history feel like the most boring subject, when in fact history is crazy interesting and pretty dramatic.

Like, this could be the most fun and amazing college to attend in the whole entire state, but the tour didn't make me excited about this school for Gabby at all.

My family looked pretty into it, though.

I guess I was missing something.

We'd been on our feet for more than an hour, oohing and aahing at building after building.

Which all looked pretty much the same, if you ask me.

Mostly I found my eyes being drawn away from the human structures toward the oak trees scattered all over the sprawling campus.

Maybe to everybody else the trees all looked the same, as similar as the buildings seemed to me.

But for me, each tree had something unique about it.

Something a lot of people don't know about me is that I adore trees.

They feel like a distant family to me.

They were my angels every summer at camp, where I would walk in the woods alone every day.

On those walks, I would greet the trees and touch their trunks and even press my face against them.

Like, I'd be legit telling them my business and asking them for advice about certain things.

I don't know how to explain my connection to trees except that I felt like I was being listened to.

I was amazed by their long trunks and branches, twisting up toward the sky.

I imagined that if trees could talk, they would be so wise.

I always felt better after chilling with them.

One time at camp, a girl from my own cabin caught me with my forehead smooshed against my favorite willow and looked at me like I was such a weirdo. I swear I wanted to crawl under a rock, never to be seen again!

Donut Delivery!

When she asked what I was doing, I didn't know how to explain it. I think I babbled something ridiculous, like that putting your forehead against a tree was good luck.

I didn't think I'd get away with it, but suddenly she put her forehead against the tree too!

I didn't want people to think something was wrong with me, but I didn't want to stop, either.

So I started waking up early in the morning before anyone else (I arranged it with one of the counselors—I'd tell her when I was leaving for my walk and report to her the minute I returned.)

Then I'd have my private heart-to-heart with the trees.

I swear, in thinking about that time at camp, my heart wanted to hug every single tree on this campus.

I didn't get to spend too much time with trees in Bellgrove.

Then I laughed to myself just thinking about the kinds of looks I would get from folks if I started hugging the trees here—especially my sister!

I honestly couldn't wait until this tour was over so we could be free to explore as we wanted.

Building after building, and we hadn't ventured inside a single one yet.

We stopped in front of a dome-like building that looked almost like an enormous extraterrestrial beetle, with nothing but windows. It looked super modern, almost futuristic.

"This is the newly renovated freshman center, where freshmen can see their counselors and just hang out or study," the tour guide explained.

I rolled my eyes as a wave of excitement rippled through the crowd at the sight of the state-of-the-art building, which the guide told us the school had raised a ton of money for.

Their commitment to making freshmen feel comfortable, I guess.

It did look like a pretty cool building, newer than the brick structures most everywhere else.

I was starting to get more interested in what was going on inside all the buildings.

I knew it was spring break and everything, but if only we could sit in some of those classes!

I wanted to experience what kinds of things the college students were learning . . . and doing!

I wondered if college classes were anything like

middle school ones. Were the students like adults or did they text each other behind their professors' backs and giggle, too?

Not far from the beetle-like building was a queenly oak tree that looked perfect for sitting.

With all these tree bodies and human bodies everywhere, the itch to start sketching should have been out of control by now.

But something else was starting to take over my mind. A different kind of itch.

A literal itch.

Spreading all over my legs.

Like a wildfire!

The scratchiness had started coming on at the beginning of the tour, but it was so subtle, I didn't pay it much mind . . . at first.

When it started coming on stronger, that was when things got super awkward for me.

Have you ever tried scratching your calves while walking without anyone noticing?

At first, rubbing my calves together as I walked started to slow me down. Finally, I drifted to the back of the crowd and started scratching my legs vigorously.

What was happening to me?

What should I do?

"Are you enjoying it, Casey? Quite some history to this campus, eh?" my dad said, his voice at my back.

I froze, then straightened up.

He must have thought that I'd fallen back from them out of lack of interest with the whole scenario.

"Yeah, I actually feel super inspired by the trees to make my first sketch," I said, patting my messenger bag, and pointed at the tree next to the freshman center. "Can I post up at that tree for the rest of the tour?"

My dad glanced into the crowd, but there was no sign of Mom or Gabby, who were probably right up front.

"Have a ball. We'll find you there after," Dad said. "And Casey, thanks for being such a good sport. I know it really means a lot to your sister."

"Thanks for checking on me," I said.

I watched him walk back to the front of the crowd and disappear into it.

Breathing a huge sigh of relief, I made a beeline for the grandmother oak tree and leaned up against it as I rummaged through my messenger bag for lotion.

I squirted the travel-size bottle up and down my shins.

That was when I noticed these red splotches all over them!

Almost like a rash!

What was happening to me?

My shea butter lotion hardly worked for long.

I still wanted to scratch the mess out of my legs; the urge just wasn't as intense.

Speaking of lotion, I was pretty sure that Gabby's magic cream was the culprit.

I remembered when she said that I would either slap her or thank her for what she did.

At first I'd wanted to thank her.

Now I wanted to . . .

Well, I definitely owed her one!

My legs were really starting to act up again.

I quickly found out that the tree's bark was smooth yet textured enough to give me some relief without scratching my skin raw!

OMG, I must have looked like such a weirdo, but I didn't care at this point.

It felt too good hugging this grandma tree, my forehead against it, calves rubbing against it.

"What's the best way out of this?" I asked the tree.

I closed my eyes and listened for an answer.

One word came into my head then.

Honesty.

I suddenly heard a familiar voice behind me.

It made me jump.

"Casey!" a boy's voice said. "I've been looking for you all over this big campus. I should have known I'd find you hugging on some tree."

Huh?

Before turning around, I was sort of confused, because this boy's voice was so out of place.

I was transported for a moment to another embarrassing day at camp when I was spotted hugging a tree by none other than . . .

Chapter Six
Dad to the Rescue

"MATT?!" I said, turning around.

I couldn't believe my eyes.

"What's up, Casey," Matt said.

Definitely him.

Those eyes.

That smile.

And voice.

There was no mistaking it.

Time slowed down, and my heart sped up.

What with being so tangled up in this college tour drama, I'd been too preoccupied to think about Matt much.

Which was exactly what I wanted, actually.

"Are you for real?" was all I could manage.

Irony.

Just as I was starting to forget my camp crush, here he was!

It was like he magically appeared in front of me from so many hours away.

I really and truly couldn't believe my eyes!

How was this possible?

I was so confused.

Months had passed since the previous summer, when I'd last seen Matt in person.

He was looking even better in person.

He was a little taller now, and he had decided to grow his bushy brown hair out of his neat Caesar cut into his own biracial rendition of a 'fro.

I stared at him in disbelief, feeling every which way: mortified, thrilled, shocked.

I almost forgot that I was in the middle of a crisis!

"I'm no tree, but can I get one?" he said.

His arms were out.

I opened my arms, and he stepped into them and lifted me off the ground for a brief instant.

The hug was short and warm, and he smelled clean, like pine.

He gave me the once-over and smiled.

"I've never seen you look so girly. And I see you've gone public with the tree-hugging thing," Matt said.

He grinned slyly.

How could I forget the day he'd spied on me hugging an old sycamore deep in the woods when I thought I was alone?

Who knew how long he'd been spying before he crept up behind me and roared like a bear, scaring the heck out of me!

Anyhow, that was when Matt found out about my secret love for trees, three weeks into our friendship.

Not even Lindsay knew about this side of me.

Now I would have to tell her in order to tell this crazy story.

Hopefully she wouldn't be so upset to learn of yet another thing she never knew about me.

No more beating around the bush about my tortured legs; it was time to just be real.

"I can't help it, I'm struggling right now," I said. "Look, I'm surprised and happy to see you and everything, but I'm in crisis mode here!"

"You are?" Matt said.

"Do I look happy to you?" I asked him.

"I guess you don't look as happy to see me as I was to see you," Matt said.

His smile fell just a tad.

"Not your fault. It's my legs. It's like they're screaming," I said.

He squatted beside my legs to give them a good look.

The red splotches were definitely visible to the naked eye at this point as they started to take over my whole shin and calf area.

"Ew. I hope it's not contagious," Matt said, touching one of my shins gingerly with his index finger.

"Matt!"

"Just kidding. Sit down," he said.

I sat on the grass next to him, and he started to rub my legs quickly up and down to give them some relief.

"What gunk did you put on your legs to make them so angry?"

"How'd you know?" I said. "And it wasn't me, it was Gabby!

"She spread lotion all over my legs and told me

to keep it on for ten minutes, then wash it off.

"I admit I got caught up and probably kept it on for a little longer.

"Anyway, when I rinsed it off, poof, no leg hair!"

Matt let out a laugh that told me there was a story behind it.

"Oh, Gabby got you with the hair removal cream. My stepsister Clare tried that stuff once, and she had this same allergic reaction."

"Oh no! So what should I do?" I started to panic.

Then I remembered to just pay attention to my breathing to anchor myself.

This was no situation for getting too carried away.

I peered at the shrinking crowd nearby as the tour was coming to an end.

My family was still lingering in front of the freshman center.

My dad was taking pictures with his camera phone and talking to some man next to him. Gabby was talking to this curly-headed girl with a fantastic smile and bright sneakers.

I squinted to see that my mom was giving a woman a hug.

I hadn't seen her hug anyone like that since Amy Cooper.

The woman looked exactly like . . .

"Hold up. Is that your mom hugging my mom?" I asked.

I was amazed at the scene unfolding right before my eyes.

I now recognized the girl in the bright sneakers.

"And my sister fist-bumping your stepsister? When did our families become so buddy-buddy?"

"Yeah, about that," he said, face-palming himself. "Remember weeks ago when your mom asked for my mom's number?

"Once they realized our sisters were the same age and would be looking into schools around this time, our moms have been discussing this meetup on the low ever since."

"And you didn't even think to tell me?" I almost shouted.

I couldn't believe the deception that had been going on behind our backs.

"Hey, I only found out an hour ago, when we got here!" Matt said. "As soon as I did, I've been all over this campus looking for you."

He laughed out loud then, like he still couldn't believe his eyes either.

We had been lied to for weeks!

No wonder I'd gotten the memo so late; that was no accident.

It was probably so I wouldn't have time to spill the tea to Matt about the trip in a text message.

This meant that Gabby knew that I was going to see Matt today.

Knowing her, I was sure she was probably bursting to tell me everything.

It made me wonder who else knew.

Lindsay?

All of Bellgrove?

I fumed.

I sure was impressed . . . not to mention betrayed! Especially by Gabby.

Come to think of it, I had noticed yesterday that she kept stressing me about choosing my wardrobe carefully for this trip.

Her subliminal messaging was probably the reason why I'd decided to slide on this girly skirt in the first place.

I couldn't help but appreciate how cool a big

sister Gabby was for trying to help me solve my leg-hair problem before running into my crush.

Only to end up with raspberry legs in front of said crush.

I had to admit, I wanted to both thank her and slap her.

And I'd never felt so happy and so mad at the same time.

I just wished I wasn't in such uncomfortable agony!

I started to twitch from the discomfort.

"Poor Casey Case," Matt said, tsking.

His smile died off as he started to move his hands up and down my legs again.

It helped to distract me from the itching.

"I'm sorry to break it to you, but this definitely calls for a pharmacy trip by one of the adults. They have an over-the-counter cream for this."

I groaned.

"I was hoping that it wouldn't have to come to that," I admitted.

I explained my dilemma to Matt, the bit about not having actual permission to shave my legs, which technically still never happened.

I mean, I used Gabby's "magic cream" but still had not taken a razor to my legs.

"The last thing I want to do is make my personal problem public knowledge, while throwing my sister under the bus in the process!" I explained.

"I feel you, but Gabby'll be aight!" said Matt. "She knew what the rules were, and she knew what she was doing even if you didn't.

"This is about you feeling normal again. That's what's most important here."

"I guess you're right," I said.

"Plus, isn't your dad the coolest doctor this side of the state? He's probably a traveling pharmacy!"

I wanted to kick myself.

My dad always traveled with his doctor bag in case of any emergency.

I thought about my last conversation with my dad and felt like such a loser.

I should have asked for his help earlier when he came to check on me. I should have just opened up to him, of all people, when I had the chance.

What was I so scared of, anyway?

It wasn't like I'd technically done anything so wrong by going along with Gabby, had I?

And even if I had, what was the worst my parents were going to do to me for defying one of their most irrational rules ever?

"I was overthinking the whole scenario and didn't let my dad help me when I had the chance," I said.

"Uh-oh. Well, here's your second chance," Matt whispered.

He took his hands off my legs and stood up.

"Good day, Mr. Peters," he said.

"Dad?!"

I turned around to see my dad standing behind us. He looked really displeased.

"Hello, Matt. Hi, Casey. Sorry to interrupt," my dad said calmly. "But what's the meaning of this, you two?"

I wasted no time in bringing my dad up to speed about the whole situation.

He look relieved once he learned that I in fact hadn't come on a college tour just to get my legs touched in broad daylight by some boy.

Once he got over that part, his face grew serious as he knelt down to inspect my poor flaming legs.

I hardly ever got sick or sprained muscles like

my ballerina sister, so I never really got to feel what it was like to be one of my dad's patients.

It was one of those things that I always wondered about but never wanted to actually find out.

I don't do pain or illness very well.

But I must say, it felt nice to have his humongous hands cupping my calves like a cradle.

This must have been what it meant to be in good hands.

By now it was clear that I had an all-out rash.

Gross.

It was starting to look like someone had mushed raspberries all over my legs.

If my skin had been white like Lindsay's, it would have stood out so much more, but since I wasn't as chocolatey as my sister, it was still pretty obvious.

At least to me.

"Matt, do me a favor and keep the crowd distracted if it becomes necessary while I get this under control?" Dad told him.

"Yes sir!" He bolted off.

Dad told me to sit tight for a few minutes as he went back to the car to get his doctor's bag.

He was back in a flash.

"This rash has become pretty inflamed, Casey. You saw me a little while ago. Why didn't you speak up then?" Dad asked me.

He opened up his leather black bag.

"It wasn't as intense as it is now, but I still pretended like nothing was wrong when you were around," I confessed.

I sighed.

"I was hoping that it was something I could figure out on my own, without involving everyone . . . including you. Sorry, Dad."

"Don't apologize to me. You put yourself through some needless suffering," Dad said.

He chuckled.

"But I can definitely relate to wanting to handle my own situations sometimes.

"It's just not always the best idea, or even realistic. You have to use your intelligence to know when to ask for help, Casey.

"Luckily for you, I have everything you need to feel a little better."

"You're right, Dad," I murmured.

He got some alcohol wipes and began to pat my legs with it.

It burned so bad I wanted to scream.

"I know the feeling—every time I put on aftershave," he said.

I cringed. "Ouch."

Next, he pulled out a yellow tube of clear ointment and rubbed the goop up and down my legs.

Finally, the intense itching sensation began to fade into a memory.

"Thanks, Dad," I said, feeling pretty ashamed of myself.

"We'll be in good company for the rest of today," Dad said.

He gestured to where the remaining families lingered near the freshman center.

I could now really appreciate the peacefulness of the campus, with its spring blossoms everywhere.

"Would've been nice to know," I muttered.

"Seeing that I went with the flow, I apologize because I can now say I agree," Dad said. "Most times, it's better to be prepared than surprised."

"Gabby tried to prepare me the best way she knew how, I suppose," I said.

I looked down at my legs.

"That's the way that cookie crumbled," Dad said, He shook his head.

"Well, it's on you to talk to your mother about everything when the time's right. I'm staying out of this one."

"Thanks again, Dad," I said. "You're my hero, not just the whole town's."

The smile on my father's face then was enough to light up a night sky.

Chapter Seven
A Magical Day

Gabby was the first to spot me and hunt me down when Dad and I returned to the fray a few minutes later.

It was midafternoon by that time, and the sun was on its westward walk across the sky.

Our families were still congregated in front of the freshman center.

"Surprise," Gabby said.

She had a sheepish look on her face.

"Sorry I couldn't give you a better heads-up, Case. Mom swore me to secrecy."

"I figured as much," I muttered.

"I would've loved to see the look on your face when you first saw him, though," she admitted.

"Well, the whole moment was ruined, thanks to you," I snapped.

Gabby looked surprised and opened her mouth to say something, but Mom was swiftly approaching.

"How do you like your surprise, Case?" Mom asked, approaching me carefully.

She also looked a little guilty.

I must've been wearing my annoyance on my face big-time!

Soon enough, everyone else began to gather around to listen in.

"I just don't understand why it had to be a surprise," I said.

"Well, Case—" Mom started to say.

"It was my idea," Mrs. Machado said, coming into the growing circle. "Hey, Casey dear.

"It's so nice to see you, but you do look displeased, and I want to take responsibility for my part in it.

"It was my idea to surprise Matt in this way, and I convinced your mom to go along with it. Which meant making it a surprise for you, too.

"My apologies if it made this day uncomfortable for you in any way."

Was Mrs. Machado for real?

My assistant principal mom, caving into . . . peer pressure?

I couldn't wait to tell Lindsay!

"Well, I wasn't exactly a puppet on a string," Mom said to me. "It's true that arranging this surprise wouldn't have crossed my mind, but once Patricia presented the idea, I thought, why not add a little spice to this occasion?

"I like surprises, and I thought you would too."

When did you *start liking surprises?* I wanted to say to her, but I kept quiet.

Gabby grinned and rolled her eyes at me because she knew that Mom was on a roll.

"I would have been surprised if you told me . . . back in Bellgrove," I insisted.

"Then I stand corrected," Mom said.

"Well, I was all for the surprise," butted in Clare.

"More like a shock to my system!" I muttered. Now that got a few laughs.

"Come on, Case, where's your zest for life?" Gabby teased.

She and Clare were linking arms like true besties.

I was amazed that all these friendships between our families were blossoming behind our backs.

I felt like I was in the twilight zone.

I wondered if Matt felt the same way.

Matt drifted to my side then, but not exactly to my rescue.

At least not right away.

I noticed that he was actually being pretty quiet once we were around everybody.

I wondered how he was feeling about the way his family had done things.

This surprise had been forced on him, too, after all.

Did he appreciate his mom's plan carried out to perfection, or would he have preferred a heads-up too?

"And how about you, Matt?" Clare asked him. "Are you happy to see your Casey Case?"

"Clare!" he groaned, looking embarrassed.

Umm . . . did she just out him to everyone on his secret pet name for me?

How sweet! I thought, blushing.

I could feel my lips twitching with a swallowed smile.

I was going to like this learning-about-Matt-through-his-family thing.

Donut Delivery!

Matt sounded sincere when he answered, "Of course I'm hyped to see Casey. She's my girl.

"I just wish I'd known I was going to see her before leaving the house. I would have brought something for her."

"Ooh, that's so sweet, isn't it, Casey?" Gabby said in an obnoxious singsong voice.

She elbowed and winked at me.

I just about died of embarrassment.

Where was Lindsay when I needed her?

She would have saved me from this humiliation.

Cringing and swooning, cringing and swooning. Matt's sharing put me into another frame of mind.

I couldn't help but wonder what he would have brought for me from his hometown if he had known he was going to see me today.

I made a mental note to ask him later.

"Well, now that everything's settled, let's eat!" said Mr. Machado.

"My man," my dad said to him, offering his fist for a bump.

Matt and I met eyes.

We had to find a way to lose the rest of these embarrassing people as soon as possible.

The question that stood between us was how.

Now this was what I would consider a big-sister-to-the-rescue-type moment.

And thank God Gabby came through.

Because did the adults really expect us to spend the entire time with them?

"Well, you adults go enjoy some eats," Gabby said smoothly. "We'd rather wait to eat until dinner. Right, Clare?"

"Oh yeah, food is the last thing on my mind," Clare smartly replied.

"We want to stay and rub our noses in this beautiful campus for a few more hours! Don't we, guys?" said Gabby.

Matt and I nodded.

"The kiddos can tag along and we can meet up with you old folks later for dinner."

"Well, if that's how you want it," Dad said, before turning to the rest of the adults. "Shall we geezers hobble on over to the closest eating spot?"

The adult crew chuckled with Dad.

"Forget the closest. Go for the best," Gabby said.

She handed him a map of town with stickers on the eating places with the highest reviews.

It was good of Gabby to have put in all that time researching the hot spots for every town on our itinerary.

However, the maps and cutesy stickers went a little overboard, in my opinion.

"But don't you—"

"I've already memorized it, Dad," Gabby said. "Plus, we could always map your location on my phone and meet you guys wherever you are at, let's say six o'clock."

"Okay," Dad said slowly, nodding.

He was balancing his sensible side with his overprotective side on some scale inside his mind.

Usually Mom and Dad would make these decisions together, but Dad was actually the only parent who seemed concerned about us at the moment.

Mom and her new BFF were chatting and laughing it up, as Matt's stepdad looked on, silent and grinning.

It was a cool vibe.

"We'll be fine," Gabby said. "The tour guide is still here, and we want to ask more questions before taking off."

"All right, off we go," Dad said, waving. "Stay close to each other and take care."

We said our goodbyes and watched our parents drift away.

As soon as they were out of sight, we let out a collective sigh of relief and dang near threw a party with no food or balloons!

"Okay, you two," Gabby said to me and Matt. "Meet me and Clare right at this spot in two hours. Then we'll roll together to meet the fogies for dinner."

"Huh? Okay," I said blankly.

"Byeeee," our sisters said.

And just like that, Matt and I were completely alone.

I stood for a few seconds, feeling dumb and amazed.

It was literally like a prayer being answered before my eyes.

I made a mental note not to slap Gabby later.

After her recent smooth move that freed us all, the itchy leg drama was officially water under the bridge in my book.

"So where do you want to go?" Matt asked.

"Absolutely nowhere," I said, laughing. "At least not right this minute. What about you?"

"After all that time I spent turning this campus upside down looking for that cute face of yours? Please, where do we sit?" Matt laughed.

I couldn't help but laugh too.

"But seriously, I don't care what we do or where we go," Matt declared. "I just want to have a college experience . . . with you."

My face temperature must've gone up a few degrees.

"Explain 'college experience'?" I asked.

"I don't know. Haven't you ever wondered what it's like to be one of . . . them?" Matt asked.

We fell into our own pools of thought as we looked silently around at all the college kids milling about—well, the ones who'd stayed behind for their spring break week.

Maybe that was why no one looked like they had a care in the world.

Just going on their way and minding their business, most of them on their phones as they walked or lounged on benches and under trees.

Even though Matt and I must have looked like

hobbits to everyone else, no one paid us any mind.

I tried to imagine this campus in full swing with four times this number of students, just rivers and seas of students everywhere.

"Think about it, Case," Matt said. "No one knows us here, and no one cares. For just an afternoon, we can be anyone we want to be."

Ah, I understood what he was saying now.

Role-play.

Like we did in our camp theater class.

"So what was your major again?" I asked Matt, falling into character.

"English with a creative writing emphasis," he answered without missing a beat.

He gave me his most winning smile.

"Let me guess. Architecture major?"

We both laughed, because it was clear that I had no interest in the buildings on this campus.

"Close. I'm majoring in art."

Oh my, that felt so good to say. And oh so real.

Something amazing happened then.

It was like years passed by in just seconds, and Matt and I were now college kids.

Which meant old enough and away from home

enough to be who we wanted to be. To each other.

"Art major sounds like you," Matt said.

He surprised me by catching my hand as we walked and then holding on to it.

I mean, he didn't even let go!

Wow.

My first time holding hands with any boy. But I wasn't sure if it was him holding my hand or the college kid he was pretending to be.

His hand felt warm and soft.

"So what have you been working on?" he asked. "Any new drawings you want to show me?"

"You really want to know?" I asked. "To be honest, I've been so busy with schoolwork I haven't had time to do anything artistic.

"I swear I feel half zombie inside. Middle sch—I mean, college is not easy."

"Good save," Matt said softly, with a chuckle. "Well, it's the same story with me and my writing. I try to sling some ink every day, but school's been wearing me out and I'm missing days in between."

Slinging ink.

Matt's way of naming what he loved to do most: write.

Matt's been writing a book about his life since he started writing at five. The way his mom tells it, he was born with an invisible pen in his hand, a born writer.

Matt's goal was to become a published author as a teenager.

I admired his ambition, no lie.

"Well, I packed my art supplies, hoping to get inspired this week," I said, patting my favorite army-green messenger bag.

"Why wait?" Matt said, stopping for a moment. "If you could draw anything on this campus, what would it be?"

Besides you? I wanted to say.

Instead, I pointed to the majestic grandma oak tree near the freshman center, where he'd first found me.

"I'd draw her," I said.

I loved the way her gnarled branches fanned out and twisted skyward. How she wasn't afraid to take up her space on this campus.

I was secretly relieved to know that Matt was cool with pressing the pause button on all the walking and gawking for a little while.

"Sounds like a plan, girlfriend.

"Let's sit somewhere and draw you a tree," said Matt, squeezing my hand, which he hadn't let go of yet.

"Girlfriend, hmm? Is that why you're holding my hand?"

"Just playing my part . . . in being who I want to be," Matt said with a mysterious smile.

"And who would that be?" I asked, curious.

"I guess I'm still sorting through that," he admitted.

Even though he looked me in the eye, his smile looked shy.

I didn't admit it then, but I was too.

Sorting through my feelings, that is. Let's say I actually was allowed to have a boyfriend in middle school . . . would I even want one?

Did I even have time for one?

What did it mean to have one?

Besides, Matt's schedule was even crazier than mine, and he hardly had his phone on him because his mom did not play when it came to his schoolwork.

Imagine having a boyfriend living ten hours away without access to his phone most of the week!

Part of me thought a long-distance relationship could be kind of beautiful, but mostly it felt pretty pointless and lame.

Say if I decided to ignore these facts and just do it. If Matt became my boyfriend starting tomorrow—how would that actually change things between us?

And were we really ready for anything to change at all?

Wouldn't it be better to keep getting to know each other like friends?

If it isn't broke, don't fix it . . . right?

In the conversation between my head and heart, my head said there was no good reason to stop being just friends.

But my heart wanted something more . . . but what?

We drifted into this supermodern sculpture garden close to the freshman center.

We weaved between colorful twisted pieces of metal and found a comfy enough spot that would give me a perfect vantage point for sketching my newest subject.

Being my first tree and all, I already knew that this drawing was going to be deeply special, especially with the memory of being surprised by Matt attached to it.

"How are your legs feeling now?" Matt asked, as if reading my mind.

"Normal, almost like nothing happened," I said.

We found a simple stone bench, and I whipped out my sketchpad and pencil.

"Go dark," Matt said.

It was code for going silent, something we could do from time to time when we were together without it being all awkward.

At camp last summer, I would need to go dark while sketching. The skills I was learning in my camp's art class were all so new to me that it needed all my concentration.

Now that I was more confident, that had changed.

Also, after starting to make sketches at the field hockey games for our school website, I've gotten more comfortable with drawing in hectic environments.

I started the outline of the tree.

"So what would you have brought for me from home if you knew you were going to see me?" I asked him.

"I dunno!" Matt blurted out, with a sudden laugh. "But I'm sure I would've come up with something!"

I laughed with him, at the realness of it all.

"Well, I know exactly what I would've brought for you," I said, and left it at that.

My mouth watered at the thought of the box that still held eight donuts (we all had one on the drive up) in our car's backseat.

"You're such a tease," he said.

Speaking of donuts, I hadn't eaten in a while, and my stomach was beginning to talk to me as the sun slowly started to descend from its invisible ladder in the sky.

Matt had brought out his black notebook to do some writing while I sketched.

"Was this what you meant by a real college experience?" I asked.

Matt chuckled. "Not exactly. It feels more like summer camp all over again, to be honest."

I slammed my notebook shut and stood up.

"Then let's find our college experience!" I said, and took off.

We had a little over an hour of freedom left to

make something happen before it was time to meet our sisters in this same spot.

Matt caught up with me.

"Where are we going?" he asked.

"Shh."

I put a finger to my lips and held his hand.

It was my turn to lead the way.

Chapter Eight
Acting the Part

Our last hour of freedom flew by. Time flies when you're having fun, I guess.

Matt and I ventured into some of the different buildings, weaseled into empty classrooms, and sat inside them, imagining what it would be like to actually learn here.

One thing I didn't expect was for college classrooms to come in so many different shapes and sizes!

Some had stadium seating with hundreds of seats, with a stage at the front.

Others were regular rooms, seating thirty or so. All the rooms had whiteboards and windows. Some whiteboards carried leftover notes from instructors.

Donut Delivery!

Sometimes we had no idea what they were scrawling on about: words in different languages, equations, flowcharts, names and dates.

Also, I noticed the classrooms weren't homey like the ones at Bellgrove Middle School, which are bursting with color from posters and decorations all over the walls.

These classes seemed pretty impersonal, almost like they didn't belong to one teacher or subject.

Back at camp we took this theater class where we played all these exciting acting games and did role plays. Well, that hour of going in and out of classrooms was like one epic acting exercise.

Matt kept me on my toes by acting like a different person every time we walked into a new room, and I would have to adapt by creating a different character too!

In the biology lab, we were lab partners, where we told phony dorm stories and complained about imaginary tests and messy roommates as we dissected an invisible frog.

In another room we were perfect strangers who liked each other but didn't know how to say how we felt.

Sound familiar?

In one room Matt pretended to be a writing professor and I was a ditzy student who only wanted to twirl her hair.

He got seriously mad. It was crazy fun!

Too bad all the art studios—the spaces I wanted to spend the most time inside—were locked tight!

I wondered if they looked anything like my art teacher Mr. Franklin's room, which had our art on display, literally from ceiling to floor.

Anyhow, my favorite part was when we stumbled into a small theater.

What else was there to do but pretend to be leads in our own made-up play?

We invented a whole story on the fly and performed for a room of ghosts.

In this play, we were married and having an argument about our rebellious pet toucan, Testy (best name I could come up with at the time).

My character loved Testy the toucan, but her husband hated the bird and wanted it gone.

Testy was testing his patience with his adorable squawking sounds. He also liked stealing our food and pooping on my husband's head.

I had an absolute blast throwing pretend dishes across the room when he threatened to make my toucan Testy disappear one day.

I—I mean my character—legit lost it.

I didn't realize I could like toucans so much.

In a later scene, when it was time for the husband and wife to make up, just as Matt was leaning in to give a kiss of apology,

I noticed the digital clock on the wall and gasped.

"Oh no, we're twenty minutes late meeting Gabby and Clare. They're going to strangle us!" I said.

"Uh-oh!" Matt said.

We rushed out of the theater, down the steps, and across campus, back to our initial meeting spot, just as our sisters were strolling up, cool as cucumbers.

"Did you have fun, kids?" Gabby asked.

Matt and I looked at each other and grinned.

"It was aight!" we said at the same time.

"Okay, we're supposed to meet the parents at this amazing Vietnamese spot soon, so let's boogie," Gabby said, setting the pace.

I still couldn't help wondering what that kiss from Matt would have felt like.

What if I hadn't destroyed the moment to meet up with our sisters, who turned out to be just as late as we were?

And where was he about to kiss me?

I wasn't so sure where he was aiming.

I trusted that he would have been pretty professional about the whole thing if it came down to it.

The thing about acting, I remembered learning from camp, was how real it could feel.

Acting felt at its best when you didn't quite know where you ended and your character began.

Now Matt and I were back to our normal middle school selves, walking behind our sisters like dorks to go meet our parents.

Instead of outright holding my hand like he had earlier, he brushed the outside of his hand against mine as we walked.

And I knew it was no coincidence.

And I knew that he wondered about the kiss that never was too.

Chapter Nine
Family Dinner

We met our parents for dinner at a Vietnamese restaurant in town that was well known for its amazing noodles and pork buns.

The restaurant was supermodern and chic.

It looked more like an upscale diner, not like a traditional restaurant.

Thank goodness they had vegetarian options, because Matt's family doesn't eat pork and Gabby the foodie really wanted to come here.

I've never been to a Vietnamese restaurant and personally jumped at this opportunity to try something new, so I was excited, and ready with my camera and my trusty messenger bag.

So there we were, all eight of us, cozied up like

the best of friends in a big booth shaped like a half-moon in the middle of this swanky Asian eatery in the heart of this college town.

I wondered if this was where Gabby and Clare would be going to eat if they both ended up going to this college.

It was really starting to hit me in these mind-blowing waves how real Gabby's going away really was.

A year can be the blink of an eye.

I tried to keep the lump in my throat from growing by breathing deep and slow.

"You okay?" asked Matt.

We spoke in low tones.

We weren't alone anymore, and we didn't want everyone up in our business.

But what business?

It wasn't like we had anything top secret to discuss.

I nodded.

"I'm just thinking about the future," I said.

He and I were sitting shoulder to shoulder at one end of our half-moon booth.

Our fathers sat at the other end.

Donut Delivery!

In the middle: the moms and sisters.

Gabby was on the other side of me.

And no one was paying us any special attention.

We could have talked about anything for as long as we wanted to and no one would have even noticed or cared.

There was so much cross talk going on between the adults, so many jokes and stories being passed back and forth, that we couldn't keep track of who was saying what.

They were wild!

From what Matt and I gathered, it had something to do with some crazy adventure they'd had that afternoon in town with an outdoor tango competition they stumbled upon, which had a free class afterward.

They must've had a ball, because my dad's humongous papa-bear laugh that could shake the walls of our house came out a couple of times in that rather small Vietnamese spot.

At one point, his contagious laughter had the whole place cracking up.

I swear this whole experience felt like a daylong episode of that TV show, *The Twilight Zone*.

And there was my assistant-principal mom, Ms. No-Nonsense, catching fits of giggles with her new BFF, Mrs. Machado.

They were like two teenagers when they were together.

They already had inside jokes, like me and Lindsay!

To see my mom this happy was a trip. It was also pretty cringeworthy.

True story: when I laugh really hard, I can't help but snort.

Even though Matt thinks it's one of the most adorable things about me, I happen to find it so embarrassing.

Well, can you guess who passed that snort of shame down to me?

My mom!

Unlike me, she didn't care what anyone thought of it.

It actually made her laugh even more, a domino-effect snort. It was so obnoxiously cute.

When she was on a roll, Gabby nudged me with her elbow. I knew she was getting a total kick out of seeing our mom so young at heart.

Donut Delivery!

I honestly hadn't seen my mom so happy with someone else (besides my dad) since Amy Cooper.

It made me miss my own BFF right then and there.

"Well, by tomorrow, we'll be in different towns," said Matt.

He looked a little sad.

"I wonder when we'll see each other again, and if we'll get a heads-up the next time."

"Facts," I said.

I could feel my own heart droop.

"Are you returning to camp this summer?" I asked.

"Mom says it all depends on my grades and my attitude," Matt said.

He gave his mom the side-eye. I laughed.

Mrs. Machado was chatting it up with my mom and not paying us any mind.

Matt looked me straight in the face.

A lock of hair had fallen across his eye, and it took everything in me not to move it. But my hands were gooey with sweet sauce.

"Don't worry, Casey Case. I'll make it happen," he said.

Matt was right about something.

Today was all we had.

Even though I would never have expected in a million years to see him that day, it still felt like we hadn't gotten enough of this stolen thing called time.

"Casey Case, huh?" I asked. "What's that about?"

Matt blushed.

"Girl, I've been calling you that since we left camp," he said.

"To who, though? Not to me," I said.

"Basically my whole family—even some cousins," Matt admitted.

"Cousins, too!" I said.

This boy was secretly blowing my mind.

His cousins knew me as Casey Case?

His cousins knew of me at all?

"But why Casey Case, though?" I said.

Matt shrugged.

"I dunno. I guess I just like the way it sounds. Kind of singsong. I never really thought about it too deep."

Typical boy. For something he didn't give much thought to, he sure had my wheels churning.

"Real talk."

He offered his fist for a small bump, and I pressed my fist to his.

"Everything about the adult universe is weird. I think I'd like to stay in our kid universe a little while longer. What do you say, Casey Case?"

"Casey Case sounds like something you would call a little girl . . . or a baby. Am I like a baby to you?" I asked him.

"Kinda," he said. "I don't know, I just think you have this baby-like vibe to you. But . . . not in a bad way!

"It's not bad at all. And . . . not like a crybaby, but like a happy baby! You have this way of getting excited about stuff you're into.

"And you give me this safe, happy feeling, the way you feel around a baby.

"Like you'll never do anything to hurt me, Casey-Case."

That was when I noticed that our table wasn't loud anymore with all the grown folks chatting and laughing.

In fact, it was totally quiet, and Matt was the only one talking.

"What are you two lovebirds chatting about?" Clare asked, as if they hadn't heard it all anyway.

I wanted to disappear.

I grabbed Matt's hand and squeezed it under the table.

He squeezed it back.

"You don't even have to repeat, because we heard everything," Gabby said. "You're so sweet to my sister, Matt. . . ."

My dad's voice traveled from the other end of the booth, quieting everyone else.

"Well, you're right about one thing, young man," Dad said. "Casey is the baby of our family, and my baby girl. And while her mother and I have agreed that she's too young to have a, um, significant other, we do appreciate your place in her life."

"Bravo, Dad," said Gabby.

He wasn't always such a smooth operator with boys who liked Gabby, which had been embarrassing for her at times.

This time, Dad was able to sugarcoat the obvious message: you can't be her boyfriend, but you can still hang around.

"Thanks for the memo, Dad," I grumbled.

The adults laughed.

"I understand, Mr. Peters," said Matt respectfully.

And that was the end of that conversation.

"So what did you young'uns do this afternoon?" my mom asked, smoothly changing the subject.

She took a sip of her piña colada.

"We just visited buildings of interest, that's all," said Gabby. "We spent a lot of time checking out the sports center, didn't we, Clare?"

Suddenly Gabby and Clare looked at each other and broke into giggles—about what, only they knew.

"Okay, moving right along. We visited the sculpture garden and I started a drawing," I said.

I pulled my sketchpad out of my bag.

"The campus had some beautiful trees all over. This one is of my favorite tree. It's not finished, but you'll get the idea."

My sketch made its way across the table, and everyone had glowing things to say about it.

I didn't tell them that I still had a long way to go on this drawing, that this was just the beginning.

It felt good to share my art with everyone.

I'd come a long way, because a year ago, I was keeping my drawings to myself.

Maybe that was why so many people used to ask me if I was going to be a ballerina like my sister; it was because they didn't know what I loved to do.

These days, between the portraits I'd drawn that were hanging in my dad's office, and the sketches of students I submitted to the school website, I was finally being seen in my own light.

"Did you write anything today, honey?" Matt's mom asked him.

"I wrote about . . . Casey drawing the tree," Matt said.

Gabby nudged Clare and whispered something to her, and they both burst out laughing.

I could feel my face warming again.

"Sounds juicy. Care to share?" his nosy sister asked.

"Chill, Clare, chill," answered Matt.

Everyone laughed, even me.

Though I was curious to know what he'd written, I wasn't curious enough for him to read it in front of everyone right at this moment.

I was starting to burn under this spotlight now.

I excused myself for a bathroom break and got out of there fast.

Donut Delivery!

Before I knew it, Mom was right on my heels as I entered the small and empty women's bathroom, with two stalls next to each other.

"Having a good time, Case?" Mom asked.

"Today's been a blast! I don't want it to end," I said.

"I know the feeling," said Mom. "It's been a great day."

"Well, you look like you're having the time of your life with Mrs. Machado," I said.

Mom's chuckle echoed through the tight bathroom.

"Patty's a riot. She's like a sister. She reminds me of just how much I've missed Amy. It's been pretty amazing to have a new friend in my life."

"I'm happy for you, Mom," I said, and meant it.

We went to the bathroom, then met back at the sinks.

"So where did you get those smooth legs?" asked Mom, catching me off guard. "I saw them under the stall."

My face flushed.

I realized then that I hadn't given my legs much thought since the itching wore off earlier that day.

I had totally forgotten that I had no leg hair to complain about, and that this was still news to my mom.

Now that those suckers were down the drain, I realized how little difference it made in my day-to-day life, whether I had leg hairs or not.

The bathroom door opened and in walked Gabby.

I had to give it to her, her timing was what we called clutch.

Perfect.

"Hey, fam," said Gabby.

She looked at the two of us, feeling the tension.

"Mom just noticed my legs," I said.

"Okay. Don't jump down her throat just yet," Gabby said. "It was my idea."

"I'm listening," said Mom.

She didn't look as upset as I would've expected, but maybe she was in too good a mood to really get angry about this.

It wasn't like we were at home in our pajamas, where we could let things all hang out.

We were in a restaurant bathroom in a different town!

"I gave Casey my hair removal cream to use without telling her what it was going to actually do," Gabby said.

"Which resulted in an allergic reaction that had my legs on fire during the campus tour!" I said.

"Oh no!" Gabby's eyes widened, and a hand flew to her mouth.

I told them all about the intense itching—and Matt and then Dad coming to my rescue.

I could tell by her face that Gabby felt horrible.

"No wonder you said that the moment you discovered Matt was ruined," Gabby said. "I'm so sorry, Casey. That only happens to, like, five percent of people who use it."

"I'm glad your dad was able to help stop the itching," said Mom. "Makes you wonder if it was really worth it in the end, eh?"

"I'm not sure," I said, letting my eyes fall a bit.

"Well, what's done is done. This is not Gabby's first time defying me on this front. I guess she's creating a tradition of her own."

With that, Mom dried off her hands and left the bathroom without another word.

Gabby and I stared at each other with wide eyes

for a few seconds, then broke into giggles.

"Wow, did you see the vein in her neck pulsating?" Gabby asked. "She was more ticked off than she showed, but she held it together.

"Thanks to Patty, she's too glad to be too mad."

"Thank goodness!" I said. "The last thing I wanted was some bathroom family drama."

We both laughed at the thought.

"But for real, you and Matt look supercute together," Gabby said. "Clare and I are just loving it."

"Gabby!" I said, blushing. "He's my friend. Period."

"Well, he sure looks like he's into you," said Gabby. "Just saying."

My face was still burning hot when we left the bathroom.

By the time we returned to the table, everyone was looking at the dessert menu, which included banana soup and bean cakes.

It all looked very interesting to me.

"I do want something sweet, but for some reason, none of these are appealing to me," said Matt's mom.

"I agree. I don't think I'm feeling very

adventurous tonight," said Mr. Machado.

"That reminds me," my dad said. "If we want to skip dessert here, we have some sweet treats in the car from Casey's workplace—Donut Dreams.

"They're not as fresh as they were this morning, but they're the best donuts in the Midwest!"

"Ooh. Great idea, Dad!" I said.

"I've been dying to try those donuts ever since Casey talked about them," Matt said.

His family agreed, so after dinner we walked over to the parking lot and pulled out our box of donuts to eat in a close-by courtyard.

With my camera, I took a few natural pictures of everyone interacting in the well-lit courtyard before picking my treat and a bench a few feet away to eat it on.

Some things are best done sitting down.

Matt sat next to me with his donut to dig in.

"Whoa," he said, biting into one of Nans's peanut butter and jelly creations. "This donut is absolutely insane!"

"I told you," I said.

I gave him a small shove as I sank my teeth into an elderberry donut.

I must say, Nans had outdone herself with this sweet invention.

Every time I thought one of her new flavors was my favorite, she would come up with another head-splitting flavor.

The burst of elderberry jelly in my mouth was almost too much to bear, it was so delicious.

I gave Matt a bite of my donut, and he couldn't decide which one he liked more.

"They're both so different but somehow equally good," he said.

"Right?!" I said.

That was how I felt about all the flavors.

All different kinds of amazing.

"OMG . . . these are awesome!" Clare groaned. "If I lived in Bellgrove, I would be up in Donut Dreams every day!"

"I swear, these donuts are my weakness," said Gabby the health nut. "One of the worst parts of going to college is being too busy and far away to drive to Bellgrove and pick up donuts whenever I want!"

Just then an idea hit me like lightning as it came into my head.

I didn't say anything because I knew I'd want to talk about it with Lindsay first.

I decided to hold my tongue until I got back to Bellgrove and see my BFF in person.

I couldn't wait to see what she thought about my idea.

Chapter Ten
Love Notes and Love Stories

The next day was a jogger-pants-and-hoodie kind of day for me, I decided.

The sporty look felt more right for these kinds of days with all this walking.

Instead of being Miss Prim and Proper like Gabby, I just wanted to sprawl all over campus with my camera and sketchbook and not wonder about who was seeing what. We had three more area colleges to visit that week.

I got the itch to draw something on the ride from the second college and reached into my bag.

In the small pocket I found a piece of paper that I had put in there yesterday, right after the Machados and we went our separate ways.

Donut Delivery!

They were now traveling back to their side of the state, hitting a couple of schools up that way.

They promised they'd take us up on our invitation to Bellgrove for fresh donuts and lunch at our house.

I already couldn't wait for a day like that to happen.

All I could do was imagine Lindsay finally getting to meet Matt.

After scarfing down those donuts the night before, our families stood around in the restaurant parking lot, saying our epic farewells.

It was the longest goodbye ever!

Our moms and sisters were basically hugging bye and talking and hugging bye again.

Matt and I thought they looked ridiculously hilarious.

And if you checked out my dad and Mr. Machado by the end of it all, they could have been old college buddies, even though they seemed to have very little in common. Mr. Machado owned a motorcycle shop, and my dad had never even touched a bike.

Yet by the way they were carrying on, it seemed like they had a lot to talk about.

And then there was Matt and me.

Our goodbye was kind of awkward, mostly because our moms and sisters were dragging out the whole goodbye process, and we didn't exactly know what to say to each other anymore outside of *see ya!*

But this time, when one of his curls flopped into his eyes, I made sure to brush it aside so I could peer into them.

"Dude, keep your grades and attitude in check and get your butt up to camp this summer," I reminded him. "You need that scholarship. Eye on the prize, right?"

"No doubt," Matt said, with a soft smile playing across his lips.

When it was time to go for real now, he gave me this nice hug and pressed a folded piece of paper into my hand.

It caught me by surprise.

"What's this?" I asked.

"Just something I wrote," he said.

I was so surprised I didn't know what to say. I was not expecting that at all.

Then Matt moved in close to kiss my cheek before he turned around and walked behind his family to their car. Before getting into his family's car, he looked back and waved.

Even now, a day later, I could still feel the cool softness of his lips against my face.

I opened the note he'd given to me to read it again, like it was the first time.

It was a page from his notebook, what he wrote about me while I was drawing the tree.

I was amazed at how Matt described me down to every detail, things I would never have pointed out about myself.

With his words he painted me, his subject, to a T. I could see myself through his words.

Not to brag, but he talked about the sunlight hitting my brown curls just right.

He even talked about the way my other hand rested on the page I was sketching on and compared it to a hand pushing open a door to some magical world.

It was the most beautiful thing I'd ever read, and I felt so honored. It was definitely special.

I couldn't wait to text him thank you, but . . .

"What has you smiling so much?" Gabby asked me quietly in the back seat.

Our parents were singing a duet along with an oldies song off my dad's playlist.

A part of me wanted to show her Matt's amazing words.

But a bigger part of me wanted to keep this one just for me.

"Oh, nothing," I answered.

"Uh-huh." Gabby grinned.

She looked out her window at the trees flying by on the highway to our next stop.

Gabby respected my privacy, something I had really learned to appreciate about her now that I was older.

Matt couldn't say the same thing about his stepsister Clare.

He told me about a time she'd found some of his private writings and embarrassed him in front of everyone by reading from them at the dinner table!

His mom didn't let it go on for too long, and he didn't tell me what the writing was about, but it had to have been pretty embarrassing, because he stayed mad at Clare for weeks.

Now Gabby would never put me on blast like that.

Donut Delivery!

She was always an open ear if I needed her, but she never really pried.

It made me want to tell her almost anything.

I never really thought of it this way, but my sister was really my other BFF.

I truly couldn't picture my life without her presence in it, day after day.

I wondered which of the towns we were visiting this week would be the one to claim her.

Hopefully the one closest to home.

Who would be those lucky dorm mates, professors, and fellow dancers who would be seeing her every day instead of me?

After that day with Matt, things kind of went by in a blur as we hit three more colleges.

I got back into my photography groove, walking around and taking documentary-style pictures with my sister as the main subject.

She was going to love them!

Matt and I were texting on the regular now, sharing pictures of the other colleges and tossing jokes back and forth about our families.

All week he blew up my phone with donut GIFs, which made me LOL every time.

They were too corny not to be hilarious.

Funny how different things felt between us after seeing each other this time around.

To be honest, what surprised me the most was how lovey-dovey Matt was on this trip in ways that he'd never been at camp.

I'm talking about the hand holding, for one, and two, the sweet words, written and spoken.

I guess I was still letting it all sink in.

It was like his feelings got bigger when we came apart.

Isn't that why they say absence makes the heart grow fonder? Maybe the same was true for me, too.

After camp, I thought he'd straight-up forgotten about me because he hardly ever reached out, and when he did, it was in basically one-word responses to my texts.

It was low-key frustrating, not to mention confusing!

I think it was then that I realized how much I cared about Matt—when I thought he'd stopped caring about me.

And if you base it off our last hug at camp, who could blame me?

On our last day before the buses pulled off, Matt gave me this bro hug like you wouldn't believe.

You know, the stiff kind topped off with a heavy thump on the back that you would give to a choking person?

Yeah, not romantic at all.

This time his hug felt soft like warm bread.

It was also relaxed in a way, and it definitely went on for longer than three seconds!

In the SUV now, I could actually still feel that hug, as well as the small peck on the cheek.

Anyhow, the other good news about this week was that I sketched like crazy, experimenting in color as I'd planned. And it turned out the highway ride was the perfect time to make art.

After a while, I was so burned out on all the walking around with my camera that I would just pick a spot and my family would just meet me there afterward.

The fact that I was able to return to my artsy side this week was more memorable and valuable to me than any college tour or swanky restaurant.

It was like a return to myself in a way. I felt amazing!

I never wanted this feeling to die.

And I must admit, it was supercool being able to spend time with my family outside Bellgrove.

The week went by so fast that I didn't even text my BFF the lowdown on everything that happened with Matt and his family.

She must have been slammed at Donut Dreams, because she wasn't exactly texting me, either.

By the end of the week, I decided it would be best to tell her everything in person, just so I could see the look on her face.

She was going to be super surprised to find out that I'd gotten to see Matt and spend a whole day with him. And I had the pictures to prove it!

When we were done with all the tours, it was time to return to good old Bellgrove.

On our way home in a nearby town, we went to dinner at an incredible Caribbean restaurant, where we ordered a big fish, grilled and seasoned just right, along with coconut rice and sweet plantains and shrimp salad.

Now that all the college visits were over, Gabby talked about the pros and cons of each campus for most of the dinner.

I found my mind drifting off to think about everything that had happened that week.

I thought of Matt's last text, which said: miss u lots.

He had never been this open with me about his feelings before.

It felt nice to know how he felt, especially since I felt the same way.

I missed him like crazy!

"Casey?" my mom asked.

When I came back to Planet Earth, my family was staring at me.

I guess I had been quiet a really long time.

"Where'd you escape to? I was just asking how you felt about this trip overall."

"Pretty fun, right?" said Dad. "Aren't you glad we dragged you along kicking and screaming?"

We all chuckled.

"I really am," I said. "And I have a ton of new sketches!"

"Maybe we should make this college tour a tradition, just for the heck of it! It's never too early to start touring colleges regularly, Casey," Mom said.

I rolled my eyes.

"Yes, it is. I'm in sixth grade, Mom! Can I give high school a whirl first? My thing is, I'm always down for a road trip as long as we don't have to go on a single college tour," I declared.

Everyone laughed because they agreed.

We were pretty worn out from hearing about the history of all the schools and walking about ten thousand steps a day.

"Did I ever tell you girls that's how your father and I first met?" Mom asked.

"What do you mean?" Gabby asked.

"I always thought you two met at a party," I chimed in.

"Not so," said Dad, gazing at our mom. "We initially met on a freshman tour at our college!"

Wow.

This was news to us!

My parents always told us they met in school, but I had no idea they first met on a freshman tour!

Gabby and I grilled them for more details.

So they met on the freshman tour and started talking for almost the whole time, not paying attention to anything the tour guide was saying.

That was how into each other they were.

But because Dad was too shy and dorky to ask for Mom's phone number, and because Mom was too modest and old-fashioned to ask for his, they never knew how to contact each other after that.

Then lo and behold, they ended up at the same party months after school began!

The rest was history.

I guess they were destined to find each other one way or another.

My mind drifted back to Matt once again.

I mean, we technically met on the first day of camp, only to be reunited on a college tour.

I wondered if it was possible to create traditions without knowing it, at least at first.

"They remind me of you and Matt," Gabby said, turning the spotlight on me.

All week the Machados had been coming up in conversation. It was just that easy.

It really made an impression on my parents to have some fun social time with other adults.

Between their demanding careers and, well, Gabby and me, Mom and Dad basically had no lives.

Social lives, that is.

It meant a lot to them to connect with people

their age in such an instant way. They had a great time and went on and on about it.

"I wonder what they're doing right now," Gabby was saying. "I'm going to text Clare. I miss her already!"

"I noticed," I said. "How'd that happen? You two are so different!"

"We have at least one of the same interests," Gabby said.

She had a secret smile on her face that could only mean *BOYS!*

"I smell trouble," Dad muttered, shaking his head.

He and Gabby have disagreed over the years about her love of boys.

The main problem being, Dad didn't like any of the boys Gabby liked.

"Matt is a quite intelligent and very respectful boy. You got yourself a good one there," Mom said.

"A good what, exactly?" Dad asked.

He had a protective eyebrow raised.

"A bestie who happens to be a boy," I said.

"A boy who you like and who obviously likes you," Dad said.

"Well, look at us. What's there not to like?" I asked.

All of us started laughing, including Dad, who had nothing else to say about it after that.

Chapter Eleven
My Big Idea

The next day was Saturday, and it felt good to wake up in my own bed—finally!

Motels are fun for a little while, but there's still no place like home.

We'd gotten back to Bellgrove late the night before, after a long time on the road.

I was so tired I could hardly remember my head hitting the pillow.

Now I had two days of freedom to enjoy before school started back.

The first thing I did when I woke up was text Lindsay.

Guess who's back?! Wanna come over tonight? I asked.

Lindsay responded quickly with a YES!!!

Later I went downstairs to the kitchen pantry and gathered up a gang of our favorite snacks and brought them upstairs into the TV room.

I also spent some of the day doing laundry and getting my room back in order.

From the fast packing job on the way out, I'd left it like I was a tornado that hit it.

The day flew by. Before long, it was six p.m. and the doorbell was ringing.

Nans was always a stickler for getting herself and Lindsay to places on time.

I opened the door to Lindsay's big smile.

Nans was waving at me from her car before backing out the driveway.

"Hiiiii!" we shouted at the same time.

Lindsay and I squealed and hugged like I had just come home from summer camp all over again.

You know when you don't realize how much you miss someone until you see them again? That was how it felt to see my BFF right then.

"I can't wait to hear EVERYTHING!" she said.

"Girl, you are not ready for what I have to tell you!" I said.

"NO way!" said Lindsay.

I let her say a quick hello to my family before we sprinted upstairs to the TV room, where I had our drinks and snacks spread out, a perfect combination of sweet and salty.

Our favorite snack was this highly addictive mixed cheddar and caramel popcorn that used to be her mom's favorite.

Lindsay preferred the caramel popcorn, and the salty cheddar popcorn was my jam.

I popped on a movie more out of habit, because we didn't even end up watching a moment of it.

What was I thinking?

We chopped it up the whole time!

I gave Lindsay the full blow-by-blow, starting with the itchy leg crisis, and then running into Matt.

By then, there was no reason for a movie to entertain us, because my story was the grand entertainment!

Lindsay watched me like I was the screen, munching on her caramel popcorn with her eyes bugging out of her head, reacting to each part of the story like she was right there with me, seeing what I saw, feeling what I felt.

"Wait a minute . . . hold up!" she stopped me. "Are you for real? Matt was there? At the college? How is that possible?"

"That's what I thought," I said.

I went on to tell her about our moms and sisters hatching this whole plan behind our backs.

"I can't believe it!" said Lindsay. "I would have been *sooo* mad."

"Tell me about it," I said. "Actually, I've never felt that happy and mad at the same time!"

"I can't even imagine feeling those two things at once," said Lindsay.

Lindsay was such a great listener, something I really appreciated about her.

I could go on and on and she'd remember exactly what I'd said about something twenty minutes before and ask about it.

I told her every detail, down to the lock of hair that kept falling across Matt's eye.

I also showed her some of the photos I'd snapped that night in the courtyard as our families mingled around the open box of donuts from Donut Dreams.

I admit that I was a little nervous at first to talk so much about Matt considering our issues back in the fall, but Lindsay seemed genuinely excited to hear about all of it.

She loved seeing my sketches from the trip, too.

"Casey, these look like actual photographs! You're getting just as good as my mom," Lindsay said.

My heart smiled wide and a lump in my throat formed.

"Awww, bestie! That's the best compliment I've ever gotten about my art!" I said, hugging her.

"That was such a surprising story about Matt. I was not expecting to hear anything like that at all! And the itchy leg scene was straight out of a sitcom!

"OMG! Your first day alone was more exciting than I imagined your whole week would be! And I can't believe your moms went through all that just to make it a surprise for you guys.

"I understand it was annoying and all, but I also think it was kind of sweet," Lindsay said.

"I didn't really stop to think of it as sweet, but I guess you're right. Thanks, BFF," I said.

Leave it to Lindsay to give me a positive point of view.

"No doubt. So when do you think you'll see him again?" she asked.

I moved my mouth to speak, then stopped and grinned.

"Thanks to technology, I can see him anytime," I said.

I picked up my phone from the couch and scrolled for his number.

"You're calling him now? I can't believe you!" Lindsay said.

Within a minute, Matt's face popped up on my screen, smiling widely.

My heart jumped for joy.

"Casey Case!" he greeted me. "What's happening?"

"This is what's happening," I said.

I turned the phone to Lindsay, who was stifling a giggle.

"Why, hello."

Matt sounded surprised.

I was full of surprises tonight.

"Are you Lindsay, the original BFF?"

"You got that right," Lindsay said, recovering quickly. "How's it going?"

I couldn't believe it!

Lindsay was actually blushing a little.

This was going better than I'd expected.

"I was just downstairs arguing with Clare over what we should name our new dog," he said.

"Wait, you got a dog?!" I said.

"Yeah, we rescued him today from the pound. I'll send you pics. The parents left it up to me and knuckle-brain over here to agree on a name, and we're not seeing eye to eye at all," he grumbled. "I just came to my room to cool off, 'cause she was getting me so frustrated! She wants to name the dog Hank, after her first boyfriend who dumped her.

"I want to name him Arty because . . . it reminds me of you. Get it? Arty?" he finished.

Was he for real?

"Aww, that's so sweet, Casey," Lindsay swooned. She sounded just like Gabby.

"I like the name Arty! Did Casey tell you I like to call her Arty Farty?!"

"No!" Matt said.

We all started laughing so hard that I started snorting. That made us laugh even more.

And you know what?

This time I didn't even care. I was talking with my two besties in the whole world.

Donut Delivery!

Our bellies were aching like after gym class by the time Matt had to hang up.

"They're calling me back downstairs," Matt said. "I'll let you guys know how it goes."

"'Do that," I said.

"It was cool meeting you, Lindsay. Later, Case," he said.

"Byeeee!" we said, and disconnected.

"Well, I hope he wins," Lindsay said. "How do you feel about his dog being a daily reminder of you, though?"

Our laughing revved up all over again.

"I'm more of a cat person, as you know," I said. "But . . . if he thinks of me every time he calls his dog, well, I guess that's as romantic as it gets in middle school!"

We laughed some more.

Gabby breezed through the TV room, rolling her eyes at me and Lindsay.

"There they go again," she said, more to herself than to us, as she grabbed a water from the mini-fridge.

"So what did you think of him?" I asked Lindsay, when things got a bit quieter.

I knew she wasn't really that into boys, but I was curious to know what she thought of Matt.

"I can see why you like him," Lindsay said thoughtfully. "He's different from the boys around here for sure. He's also cuter than his pictures. I can't wait to meet him!"

"They said they'd like to visit Bellgrove one weekend for a full Donut Dreams experience.

"Oh, which reminds me! There's something I've been wanting to talk to you about.

"But before we do that . . . I've been dying to hear about your first week as a full-timer at Donut Dreams," I said.

"OMG, I think my ankles are still swollen!" Lindsay said.

She showed me her slightly puffy ankles.

She went on to tell me all about her long workweek at Donut Dreams.

It was the most hours she'd ever worked there in a single week, and she'd been exhausted by the end of it.

"If this is what adulting is all about, I'm in no rush!" Lindsay said.

"Facts," I said.

Donut Delivery!

I knew that Matt would agree too.

The movie ended, and we giggled at the fact that we'd talked through all of it.

"So, what did Matt's family think about the donuts?" Lindsay asked.

"OMG! That totally reminds me of my idea! This is what I've been wanting to talk to you about," I said.

I brought up the conversation our families were having over donuts in the courtyard, and how Gabby wished she could get Donut Dreams on the regular while she was away at college.

"What do you think about creating a donut delivery service for the college students in St. Louis?" I asked.

"That sounds amazing!" Lindsay said.

She looked super pumped.

"Do you think Nans would consider it?" I asked.

"Sure, but I think we should work out the details as much as we can before bringing it to her, because you know how Nans loves to ask a whole heap of questions.

"Let's be prepared!" Lindsay said.

She sure knew her grandma well.

So we talked out the details, such as Donut Dreams contacting colleges and universities in St. Louis.

We could make arrangements with any that were interested to deliver a certain number of donuts to their dining halls on a regular basis, maybe once a week.

It was definitely doable!

And it would help Donut Dreams expand.

"I can't wait to bring this to Nans! They're been looking for creative ways to expand the business. . . .

"What's more expansive than this?! Thanks to you, Donut Dreams donuts are about to become a well-known delicacy!" said Lindsay.

"Hey, what do you think of this logo I made?" I asked.

I flipped open my notebook to the page where I'd sketched a logo for the delivery service.

On one of the long drives to a school, it came to me in a dream.

It was a smiling delivery car with donuts for wheels.

"Wow, Casey! Just wow. It's cute, creative, and catchy! I can't believe you came up with this for my family. They're going to love it!" Lindsay said.

That felt great to hear, and it filled me with excitement.

We spent the next half hour munching on snacks and coming up with more ideas for the delivery service.

Next time Lindsay and I worked together at Donut Dreams, which was most likely next Friday (Kelsey had already told Lindsay she wanted Friday off), we'd present it to the Coopers.

Lindsay was going to have a hard time keeping her mouth shut about our idea, but I knew that she was a good secret keeper and could keep a lid on it.

In other words, we couldn't wait!

Chapter Twelve
Special Friends, Special Gifts

The next Friday after school, Lindsay and I headed to Donut Dreams early to present our donut delivery idea to Nans, Grandpa Coop, Lindsay's dad Mike, and her aunt Melissa. By that time, I had a more polished version of the logo, colored and everything. Everyone listened attentively to our idea.

"Well, look at that, a donut delivery service! Simply brilliant!" Nans said.

"I second that emotion. It's a wonderful idea, girls," Grandpa Coop said. "To execute this effectively would put us on the map in a way like never before."

"Casey, was this fabulous idea inspired by your recent college visit, by any chance?" her aunt Melissa asked.

"In every way," I said.

"Well, from an accounting standpoint, I will have to crunch some figures to see what makes the most financial sense, but I agree with Nans that this is a fantastic idea," her aunt said.

"You're really like one of the family, Casey," Mike Cooper said. "Thank you for coming up with all this. You too, Lindsay. I wholeheartedly agree that we should pursue it!"

Lindsay and I cheered.

All the adults had only positive things to say about our idea. We didn't even have to field any questions. Was this really happening?

My little idea, coming to life before my eyes.

During our shift that afternoon, my bright idea rippled across the whole restaurant to the different family members.

The older teenage cousins who were working that afternoon came up to us at various times to give us high fives and show their excitement for the delivery service.

By the time Donut Dreams closed at six, Melissa and Mike were hashing out the finer details, while Lindsay and I cleaned up the Donut Dreams counter.

I think I was still in shock that my idea was being taken so seriously!

My idea!

I couldn't wait to text Matt after my shift to tell him all the news.

It was his family who'd helped inspire the idea, after all.

The following weeks passed by like a cool breeze. I spent a week finessing my logo for the donut delivery service flyers, shirts, hats, and car magnets.

The older Cooper cousins jumped at the chance to deliver donuts; we just had to figure out whose car to use.

So we decided on a rotating schedule.

So much planning had gone into my idea.

Kelsey even helped add a link on the Donut Dreams website about our delivery services.

I mean, from top to bottom, the whole family was on board, and even though I had always felt like a part of their family, this really cemented that feeling for me.

Donut Delivery!

One afternoon I came home from school to find a package in the mailbox with my name on it.

The sender: M. Machado!

I took the small box, darted up to my room, and closed the door.

I opened the box.

In it were a white feather, a small jar of sand, and a red, black, and green beaded bracelet.

There was also a small card with a note written in black ink.

Hey, Casey Case,

Surprise! Remember when you asked me what I would have brought you if I knew I would see you?

Feathers are like business cards for angels, so think of it as good luck. The sand is from the shore at camp where we used to kayak.

Oh, did I ever tell you that I'm a sand collector? It drives my mom nuts!

The bracelet is just something I saw in town that made me think of you (which isn't that often or anything— j/k ha ha).

See ya,
Matt

When I finished reading the note, I wanted to roll my eyes, laugh, blush, and swoon all at the same time. I think it's safe to say that I was all in my feels!

Later that afternoon, I heard the doorbell ring and galloped down the stairs.

I wasn't sure if we were expecting any visitors, and I could hear my mom on the phone.

I opened the front door.

"Lindsay! Nans! What are you doing here?" I said, hugging both of them.

I noticed that Lindsay had a gift bag in her hand.

"Hiiii. This is for you!" Lindsay said, giving me the bag.

"It's a small token of appreciation for your major contribution to our business!" Nans added. "Thank you for all that you're doing to help Donut Dreams thrive.

"Your idea was a stroke of genius, Casey. I'm so thrilled that you came to us with it. The Coopers are forever grateful."

"And guess what?" Lindsay asked, bursting with excitement. "A local journalist saw the delivery service launch on our website and wants to do a write-up about it in the *Bellgrove Times*!

"We told her this was your idea and now she wants to interview you, too!"

Lindsay and I jumped up and down, celebrating, while Nans chuckled.

Soon after, my family caught wind of what was going on, and we all celebrated.

I was officially overwhelmed by the joy I felt.

My mom invited Lindsay and Nans into our spacious kitchen area, just a pivot from the front door.

"Now open the present!" Lindsay said.

"Say no more!" I said.

I dunked my hand into the gift bag and searching through the tissue paper for the sweetest thing I'd ever seen.

"Nans got it from a place she knows that makes all kinds of specialty snow globes," Lindsay explained.

It was a snow globe with a once-bitten donut inside. When you shook it up, down came sprinkles.

"Aww, that is so cute, Case," Gabby said.

She was clearly moved, just as I was.

Tears formed in my eyes and threatened my cheeks.

There was a card from the Coopers too.

I opened it and read it aloud.

"Casey Peters, you are a donut dream come true!"

The greatest family, the greatest friends (both male and female), and the absolute best donuts in the entire world.

What more could a girl ask for?

Life was sweet—sweeter than even the tastiest donut at Donut Dreams.

Still hungry?
Check out this first chapter from
another tasty series,

SUNDAY SUNDAES

Chapter One
Plot Twist

A hot August wind lifted my brown hair and cooled the back of my neck as I waited for the bus to take me to my new school. I hoped I was standing in the right spot. I hoped I was wearing the right thing. I wished I were anywhere else.

My toes curled in my new shoes as I reached into my messenger bag and ran my thumb along the worn spine of my favorite book. I'd packed *Anne of Green Gables* as a good-luck charm for my first day at my new school. The heroine, Anne Shirley, had always cracked me up and given me courage. To me, having a book around was like having an old friend for company. And, boy, did I need a friend right about now.

Ten days before, I'd returned from summer camp to find my home life completely rearranged. It hadn't been obvious at first, which was almost worse. The changes had come out in drips, and then all at once, leaving me standing in a puddle in the end.

My mom and dad picked me up after seven glorious weeks of camp up north, where the temperature is cool and the air is sweet and fresh. I was excited to get home, but as soon as I arrived, I missed camp. Camp was fun, and freedom, and not really worrying about anything. There was no homework, no parents, and no little brothers changing the ringtone on your phone so that it plays only fart noises. At camp this year I swam the mile for the first time, and all my camp besties were there. My parents wrote often: cheerful e-mails, mostly about my eight-year-old brother, Tanner, and the funny things he was doing.

When they visited on Parents' Weekend, I was never really alone with them, so the conversation was light and breezy, just like the weather.

The ride home was normal at first, but I noticed my parents exchanging glances a couple of times, almost like they were nervous. They looked different too. My dad seemed more muscular and was tan, and my mom had let her hair—dark brown and wavy, like mine—grow longer, and it made her look younger. The minute I got home, I grabbed my sweet cat, Diana (named after Anne Shirley's best friend, naturally), and scrambled into my room. Sharing a bunkhouse with eleven other girls for a summer was great, but I was really glad to be back in my own quiet room. I texted SHE'S BAAAACK! to my best friends, Tamiko Sato and Sierra Perez, and then took a really long, hot shower.

It wasn't until dinnertime that things officially got weird.

"You must've really missed me," I said as I sat down at the kitchen table. They'd made all of my favorites: meat lasagna, garlic bread, and green salad with Italian dressing and cracked pepper. It was the meal we always had the night before I left for camp and the night I got back. My mouth started watering.

I grinned as I put my napkin onto my lap.

"We *did* miss you, Allie!" said my mom brightly.

"They talked about you all the time," said Tanner, rolling his eyes and talking with his mouth full of garlic bread, his dinner napkin still sitting prominently on the table.

"Napkin on lapkin!" I scolded him.

"Boys don't use napkins. That's what sleeves are for," said Tanner, smearing his buttery chin across the shoulder of his T-shirt.

"Gross!" Coming out of the all-girl bubble of camp, I had forgotten the rougher parts of the boy world. I looked to my parents to reprimand him, but they both seemed lost in thought. "Mom? Dad? Hello? Are you okay with this?" I asked, looking to both of them for backup.

"Hmm? Oh, Tanner, don't be disgusting. Use a napkin," said my mom, but without much feeling behind it.

He smirked at me, and when she looked away, he quickly wiped his chin on his sleeve again. It was like all the rules had flown out the window since I'd been gone!

My dad cleared his throat in the way he usually did

when he was nervous, like when he had to practice for a big sales presentation. I looked up at him; he was looking at my mom with his eyebrows raised. His dark brown eyes—identical to mine—were *definitely* nervous.

"What's up?" I asked, the hair on my neck prickling a little. When there's tension around, or sadness, I can always feel it. It's not like I'm psychic or anything. I can just feel people's feelings coming off them in waves. Maybe my parents' fighting as I was growing up had made me sensitive to stuff, or maybe it was from reading so many books and feeling the characters' feelings along with them. Whatever it was, my mom said I had a lot of empathy. And right now my empathy meter was registering *high alert*.

My mom swallowed hard and put on a sunny smile that was a little too bright. Now I was really suspicious. I glanced at Tanner, but he was busy dragging a slab of garlic bread through the sauce from his second helping of lasagna.

"Allie, there's something Dad and I would like to tell you. We've made some new plans, and we're pretty excited about them."

I looked back and forth between the two of

them. What she was saying didn't match up with the anxious expressions on their faces.

"They're getting divorced," said Tanner through a mouthful of lasagna and bread.

"What?" I said, shocked, but also . . . kind of not. I felt a huge sinking in my stomach, and tears pricked my eyes. I knew there had been more fighting than usual before I'd left for camp, but I hadn't really seen this coming. Or maybe I had; it was like divorce had been there for a while, just slightly to the side of everything, riding shotgun all along. Automatically my brain raced through the list of book characters whose parents were divorced: Mia in the Cupcake Diaries, Leigh Botts in *Dear Mr. Henshaw*, Karen Newman in *It's Not the End of the World.* . . .

My mother sighed in exasperation at Tanner.

"Wait, Tanner knew this whole time and I didn't?" I asked.

"Sweetheart," said my dad, looking at me kindly. "This has been happening this summer, and since Tanner was home with us, he found out about it first." Tanner smirked at me, but Dad gave him a look. "I know this is hard, but it's actually really happy news for me and your mom. We love each other very much and will stay close as a family."

"We're just tired of all the arguing. And we're sure you two are too. We feel that if we live apart, we'll be happier. All of us."

My mind raced with questions, but all that came out was, "What about me and Tanner? And Diana? Where are we going to live?"

"Well, I found a great apartment right next to the playground," said my dad, suddenly looking happy for real. "You know that new converted factory building over in Maple Grove, with the rooftop pool that we always talk about when we pass by?"

"And I've found a really great little vintage house in Bayville. And you won't believe it, but it's right near the beach!"

I stared at them.

Mom swallowed hard and kept talking. "It's just been totally redone, and the room that will be yours has built-in bookcases all around it and a window seat," she said.

"And it has a hot tub," added my dad.

"Right," laughed my mom. "And there are plantings in the flower beds around the house, so we can have fresh flowers all spring, summer, and fall!"

My mom loved flowers, but my dad grew up doing so much yard work for his parents that he refused to ever let her plant anything here. The house did sound nice, but then something occurred to me.

"Wait, Bayville and Maple Grove? So what about school?" Bayville was ten minutes away!

"Well." My parents shared a pleased look as my mom spoke. "Since my new house is in Bayville, you qualify for seventh grade at the Vista Green School! It's the top-rated school in the district, and it's gorgeous! Everything was newly built just last year. Tan will go to MacBride Elementary."

"Isn't that great?" said my dad.

"Um, *what*? We're changing *schools*?"

"Yes, sweetheart. I know it will be a big transition at first. Everything is going to be new for us all! A fresh start!" said my mom enthusiastically.

Divorce. Moving. A new school.

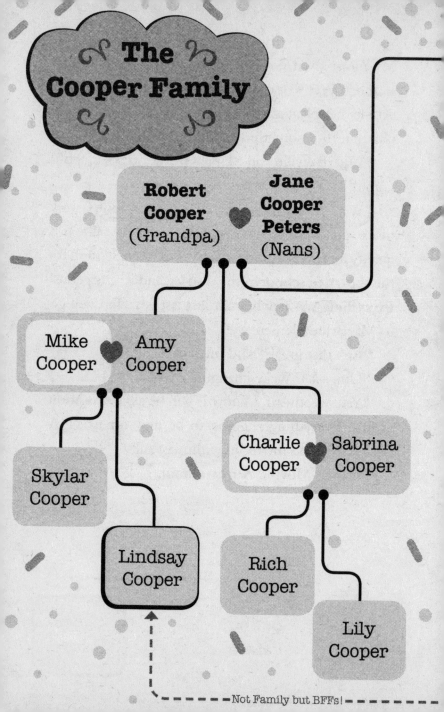

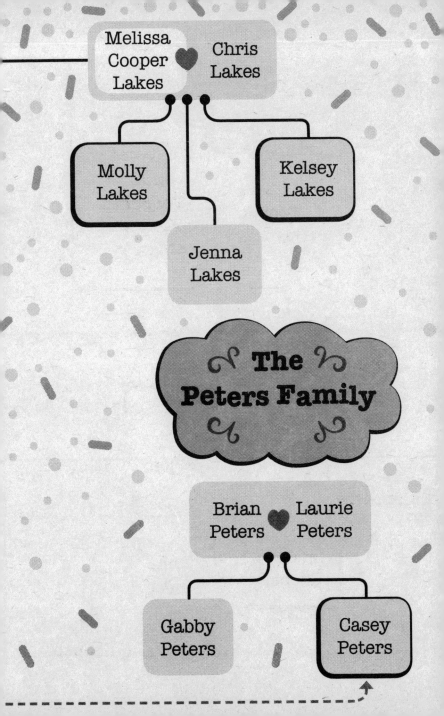